The words echoed in the sudden silence. Grant turned to face her and Sharon tilted her head, then grinned and winked.

This was Grant, her best friend, offering nothing more than a friendly kiss to seal a bargain, Sharon told herself as he slowly lowered his head. Her eyes fluttered shut; her breath caught as his lips settled against hers.

The soft, gentle kiss ended far too quickly.

She opened her eyes to meet his gaze—a puzzled gaze that clung to her lips like a touch and had her heart hammering wildly. A shimmering awareness seemed to hang between them.

Then Grant cleared his throat and stepped back.

And the moment died so quickly, Sharon wondered if she had imagined it.

Dear Reader,

Welcome to another wonderful month at Silhouette Romance. In the midst of these hot summer days, why not treat yourself (come on, you know you deserve it) by relaxing in the shade with these romantically satisfying love stories.

What's a millionaire bachelor posing as a working-class guy to do after he agrees to baby-sit his cranky infant niece? Run straight into the arms of a very beautiful pediatrician who desperately wants a family of her own, of course! Don't miss this delightful addition to our BUNDLES OF JOY series with *Baby Business* by Laura Anthony.

The ever-enchanting award-winning author Sandra Steffen is back with the second installment of her enthralling BACHELOR GULCH miniseries. This time it's the local sheriff who's got to lasso his lady love in *Wyatt's Most Wanted Wife*.

And there are plenty of more great romances to be found this month. Moyra Tarling brings you an emotionally compelling marriage-of-convenience story with *Marry In Haste*. A gal from the wrong side of the tracks is reunited with the sexy fire fighter she'd once won at a bachelor auction (imagine the interesting stories they'll have to tell) in Cara Colter's *Husband In Red*. RITA Award-winning author Elizabeth Sites is back with a terrific Western love story centering around a legendary wedding gown in *The Rainbow Bride*. And when best friends marry for the sake of a child, they find out that real love can follow, in *Marriage Is Just the Beginning* by Betty Jane Sanders.

So curl up with an always-compelling Silhouette Romance novel and a refreshing glass of lemonade, and enjoy the summer!

Melissa Senate
Senior Editor
Silhouette Romance

Please address questions and book requests to:
Silhouette Reader Service
U.S.: 3010 Walden Ave., P.O. Box 1325, Buffalo, NY 14269
Canadian: P.O. Box 609, Fort Erie, Ont. L2A 5X3

MARRIAGE IS JUST THE BEGINNING

Betty Jane Sanders

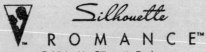

Silhouette
R O M A N C E™
Published by Silhouette Books
America's Publisher of Contemporary Romance

To Lee, always.

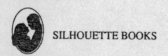

SILHOUETTE BOOKS

ISBN 0-373-19245-2

MARRIAGE IS JUST THE BEGINNING

Copyright © 1997 by Betty Monthei

Printed in U.S.A.

Books by Betty Jane Sanders

Silhouette Romance

His Secret Son #1131
Marriage Is Just the Beginning #1245

BETTY JANE SANDERS

With the publication of *His Secret Son*, a 1994 Golden Heart winner, Betty's dream of becoming a published author had come true.

Betty has lived in Alaska since 1980, with her husband of twenty-plus years. Her hobbies include spending time with her husband, skiing, snow machining, walking her dog (a springer spaniel named Brittany), hiking, biking, boating, scuba diving, reading, writing, drawing and painting.

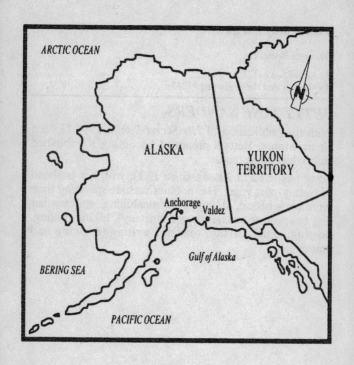

Chapter One

Six-year-old Cassie's giggles spilled down the hall, easily reaching the kitchen. Sharon paused, a plate in hand, to savor the sound. Brittany barked—a puppy yelp. It was followed by a sudden splash of bathwater. Cassie squealed, Brittany barked again and Sharon cringed. She quickly put the last of the plates in the dishwasher, then hurried down the hall.

Fragments of bubbles floated in the bathwater. Cassie had soap in her hair and brows, while foam clung to her chin like a small goatee. Brittany lay in the tub in front of Cassie, a puff of soap perched atop her head. Sharon groaned. The puppy cocked her head and cracked her jaw in a doggie smile.

Sharon fought a grin and dropped her hands to her hips, trying to scowl fiercely. "Cassie Parker! What am I going to do with the two of you?" She arched a brow at the little girl, and Cassie laughed in answer—a bubble of pure joy that filled the room. Laughing was something the child hadn't done often enough the past few months. Warmth flooded Sharon's heart at the sound.

"I didn't tell her to, Sharon. Honest. She just jumped in when I wasn't looking. All by herself."

Sharon shot a stern look at the nine-month-old springer spaniel. The dog's long ears floated on top of the water. With her bright eyes, she appeared anything but repentant. "You are hopeless, the both of you. I can't even turn my back on you for a minute," she mock-scolded.

Brittany reached over, licked the soap goatee from Cassie's chin and barked, bubbles spilling from her mouth. Cassie sputtered with laughter, then she grabbed the liver-and-white puppy to her bare chest in a hug.

"Don't be mad, Sharon. Brittany didn't mean to be bad." Her shining eyes—Grant's eyes—begged forgiveness. Just as his had countless times throughout the years, and just as easily melted Sharon's heart.

Perhaps it was her destiny to be won over by those thickly lashed Parker eyes, so dark blue they bordered on black, be it father's or daughter's. She shook her head with a sigh, leaned against the door frame, arms crossed, and just watched, as a rush of love flooded her.

"Brittany is my very best friend. I love her," Cassie declared, pink coloring her cheeks. Black hair the exact shade of Grant's slipped from where it was pinned at the top of her head.

Sharon smiled, then went to kneel next to the tub and tuck a strand of hair beneath a pin. "Well, best friends or not, we had better get her out of the tub and dried. Otherwise you won't be able to have her on the bed tonight."

As if she understood, Brittany leaped from the tub, then shook herself, spraying water and soap every direction. "Brittany," Sharon gasped.

Brittany ducked her head and woofed. Cassie snorted and choked, trying to swallow her laughter, while Sharon rolled her eyes, then grabbed a towel and began drying the pup. Then she turned to Cassie, fresh towel in hand. "Your turn, little goose."

Cassie giggled and climbed out of the tub with a splash of water and a flurry of slim arms and legs. Bittersweet warmth spiraled through Sharon at the way the little girl snuggled into the thick bath towel and leaned against her, hungry for contact from a woman and for a hug or a kiss, which Sharon happily gave. *The child needs a mother,* she thought with a sudden ache of heart. An ache that lessened only slightly when she squeezed Cassie in a tight hug, as if she were able to somehow make up for the loss.

If only she could.

She slowly released the girl and reached for a soft, flannel nightgown that swallowed Cassie, the little girl's bony ankles poking out below the hem. She stood and turned, and came face-to-face with herself in the steam-rimmed mirror.

Her thick, russet curls corkscrewed in every direction, as usual, heedless of attempts to tame them. Her round cheeks were flushed, her brown eyes wide and full of suppressed good humor.

At one time she would have grimaced and wrinkled her freckled nose in despair, but now she just shrugged with a grin. She had long accepted that no one would ever beat down the door to put her on the front of a glamour magazine, and that there were worse things in life than being plain.

Two bedtime stories and one damp pup later, Cassie raced from the living room to the spare bedroom, Brittany galloping at her heels. They jumped into bed as one as Sharon entered the room. Cassie turned with outstretched arms for a soap-scented hug and a slightly wet kiss that wrapped an iron-clad fist of love around Sharon's heart and promised no relief.

She wanted no relief.

A little over a year ago her childhood friend, Grant, had returned to Valdez with his wife, Catherine, a tall, elegant blond beauty with a cool manner. Everything that Sharon was not. And with them was their tiny daughter, Cassie, the image of Grant when he was young.

Sharon had fallen in love with Cassie, as she had fallen in love with Grant years ago. But this time it was a love eagerly returned, making Sharon ache with happiness and long with all her heart for a little girl, a child of her own. And mourn once again the fact that she would never be a mother.

She pushed the dark thought away and dropped one last kiss on Cassie's warm cheek. She left the little girl, covers pulled to her chin, whispering to Brittany, who snuggled next to her and was doing her utmost to hog the pillow.

Sharon probably shouldn't let the dog sleep there, but Brittany had been a highlight in Cassie's life in the several months since Catherine's death from cancer. So much so that Sharon had considered giving Brittany to Cassie as a gift. But her own heart had been so totally won by the puppy that she couldn't bear to part with her. Instead, she made sure that Cassie had lots of time to spend with the dog. Sharon refused to deprive Cassie of anything that made her happy.

Wind moaned around the eaves as Sharon paused at the living room window. Snow swirled and danced in the night, captured by streetlight, while naked tree branches bent and swayed with the storm.

Not the best of nights to be driving back from Anchorage, she thought, and hoped that Grant would get in soon. Three hundred miles of often winding, steep roads made more dangerous by darkness and thickly falling snow. It was hard not to worry.

He could probably make the drive with his eyes closed, she reminded herself, then pulled the drapes, able to shut the storm out but not her concern. No doubt because she had been worrying about Grant most of her life, off and on. She shook her head at the thought. Old habits were hard to break.

She flipped the front porch light on, then padded down the hall to check on Cassie. The house seemed warmer, snugger, more a home with the child there. Cassie lay on her side, one hand folded beneath her cheek, the other nesting on Brittany's neck. Nose to nose, sharing the pillow.

When she was fourteen, Sharon had dreamed of doing this very thing, except the child she would be checking on would be her own. And the father, Grant, would be at Sharon's side.

Stuff that fantasies were made of, little to do with reality, she thought with a soft smile. Even as a teenager she should have known better. It hadn't taken long to figure out that Grant, with his dark good looks, was not interested in his childhood friend. Hope died hard, but a few years later she finally accepted that he never would be hers, and she settled for friendship, instead.

Sharon shrugged memory aside and turned back toward the living room to curl on the couch in a puddle of lamplight. She pulled an afghan over her lap, book in hand, to listen to the groan and whisper of the storm at the windows. And to wait for Grant.

Thick snow swirled through the black of night, quickly adding depth to the eight inches on the ground, coating the windshield almost faster than the wipers could push it aside. A gust of wind rocked the four-wheel drive. Grant slowed his speed. January. The heart of another dark Alaskan winter that had settled with a vengeance over the land.

Not that it mattered to him. Seasons and weather were something out of his control. He had learned, while growing up, that winter in Valdez meant short days, long evenings, delayed or canceled flights, which was why he was driving back from Anchorage. There would be over three hundred inches of snow by spring if Valdez got her average snowfall. They were well on their way to the average. All a fact of life that no amount of complaining could change.

He used to look forward to winter, the first snow, skis waxed, snow machines tuned. Now the skis were covered with dust, the snow machines untouched, and likely to remain that way.

He wheeled the pickup into town, streetlamps casting light and shadow along empty streets. A neon pink-and-yellow sign flashed from a bar window, washing brilliant color across the snow. The grocery store was darkened, the parking lot vacant except for one lone, battered sedan quickly being covered with fresh snow.

Sharon's front porch light reached through the darkness in welcome. The soft glow of a lamp behind the living room curtain told him she was probably up, waiting, though he had told her not to. He should have known to save his breath.

Grant smiled in spite of himself, tension easing as he pulled into the driveway and cut the engine. He slid from the pickup, weariness fading as he strode to the front porch. The door swung open as he reached for it.

"Grant."

Sharon's voice was soft, her hair a riot of curls. Baggy gray sweats hung from her slender frame.

"You made good time. Come in. Come in."

She pulled him through the door, snow swirling behind. And reached for his coat even as he shrugged out of it, an action for both them as natural as breathing.

"Would you like some hot chocolate? I just put some on."

"Got any chocolate chip cookies?" he asked. She grinned, eyes warm with humor, pulling a smile from him in answer. She always baked cookies when Cassie was around. And they were always chocolate chip, both his and Cassie's favorite.

They headed into the kitchen together. There Sharon filled stoneware mugs while Grant piled a plate high with fresh-baked cookies. She settled across the table from him, and a comfortable silence surrounded them, broken by the murmur of the storm outside, the steady tick-tick of the kitchen clock, Sharon sipping her hot chocolate.

Grant could close his eyes and re-create the familiar scene. The sounds. The scent of her house. Sharon's soft, red-brown curls framing winter-pale skin sprinkled with freckles; the darkness of her velvet brown eyes.

Eyes he suddenly realized were fixed on him, a frown creasing her brow. He put down his mug, recognizing that look.

"Problems?" he asked, not certain he really wanted to know.

She started to shake her head, then stopped, setting her mug aside. "I'm worried about you." She held out a hand when he started to protest. "You work too much, Grant. When do you have time for fun anymore? When was the last time you *wanted* to have fun?"

The words spilled from her faster than he could stop them.

"Two sitters in three months. I know it's not your fault these women seem to think Cassie is a way into your bed and your heart, but what are you going to do, Grant? I know you are still grieving, but—"

He placed a finger against her lips. A brief touch that stopped the flow of words better than argument could.

Grieving? Yes and no, but he wasn't about to correct

her. There were some things he couldn't talk about, even with Sharon.

"I know you worry, Mom," he teased gently. "Things should slow down at work one of these days, and I will find a sitter."

As for Catherine...

The clock chimed twelve times. He hesitated, then shrugged and scooted the chair back. "I had better get Cassie and head home."

Sharon studied him briefly, shook her head with a sigh.

He knew the argument was not over. Sharon never gave up that easy.

"It's too late to argue. I'll bag some cookies for you to take," she finally said.

Grant nodded, then left her to the task.

The bedroom was dark except for the faint illumination from a night-light washing across Cassie. She was sleeping on her back, mouth slightly parted, one arm flung to the side, the other wrapped around Brittany's neck.

The pup cracked an eye, head nestled across Cassie's chest. Her tail began to thump, slow, then fast and faster, as Grant walked into the room.

He knelt by the bed and reached to touch Cassie's cheek. A soft, reverent touch. This child of his, so tiny and perfect, with a fragile beauty and a hold on his heart so strong that it sometimes terrified him.

"Daddy?" Her eyes fluttered open.

"Hello, pumpkin," he whispered.

He gently lifted her, her thin arms squeezing round his neck in a vise-grip hug that defied efforts to breathe. Breathing wasn't important. Nothing was important except for the little girl in his arms. He closed his eyes, bathed in her scent and reveled in the silken cheek pressed against his, in the warmth that rushed through him. The feeling of coming home, of rightness, when he held his daughter.

He finally relaxed the hug, then sat on the bed, Cassie in his lap, to greet Brittany, who wiggled and whined with impatience. She leaned into Grant, head planted in Cassie's lap, while he scratched behind a silken ear.

"Brittany is my best friend," Cassie said sleepily against his chest. "Except for Sharon. I love Sharon the best—no, I love you the best, Daddy. And then Sharon. And then Brittany."

Grant swallowed hard. "I know you do, pumpkin," he said in a husky voice.

Sharon waited in the living room, Cassie's small suitcase standing by the door. "I put the cookies in the suitcase," she said. Cassie bent toward Sharon, hooked a small arm around her neck and dragged her against Grant's shoulder for a goodbye kiss, while Brittany leaned into his legs.

Sharon's head stopped at his jaw. She was no taller than she'd been in ninth grade. She smelled of soap and lemon-scented shampoo, and her warmth burned through his jacket.

"I love you, Sharon," Cassie whispered loudly.

Sharon hugged back with a gentle laugh, then disentangled herself. "I love you, too, little goose." She handed Grant a blanket to wrap around Cassie.

Grant finished the task, then reached to ruffle Sharon's curls. "I owe you, once again."

Sharon pushed his hand away with a grin. "Hey, you know I spent hours fixing that do! And you know you don't owe me anything except...well, maybe dinner out next week. Chinese?" Her grin faded. "Seriously, Grant, you know I don't mind helping out. It's all part of being friends."

"Yeah, well, you've been pretty friendly lately," he said softly. "And I will be grateful if I want to."

He turned toward the door and picked up Cassie's suit-

case. "Call me tomorrow," Sharon said, then pulled the
door open and ushered them out. She stood in the glow of
the porch light, shivering, watching until they pulled out
of the drive and started down the road.

Though it was only a few miles, Cassie was asleep by
the time they drove up the hill to the house. The house he
had built to try to make Catherine happy. And now lived
alone in with his daughter.

Not that he could blame Catherine for her death; even
he could not be so heartless. But before—

Steely resolve clamped a fist on the thought and
squashed the life from it before it was completed. Grant
did not have time to wallow in the past. Streetlights
washed the other lots, empty except for four feet of snow,
before finally capturing his house at the end of the cul de
sac, standing alone in the shoulder of the mountain over-
looking town.

The few lights on in the town below seemed to flicker,
one or two here, a handful over there. Startled bursts of
yellow-white against the swirling snow, which was now
slowing, thinning to a mere flurry. Light from the Alyeska
Pipeline Marine Terminal reached from across the arm of
Prince William Sound. A faint light that stretched upward
with long, buttery fingers to brush at the dark shadows of
snow-filled mountains slowly materializing as the clouds
began to lift.

The door to the three-car garage slid open. The far stall
was filled with snow machines, snow blower and an as-
sortment of skis and garden tools, bicycles, gas grill and
lawn chairs, fishing poles and hip-waders that had cracked
from age and disuse. The other two stalls were unoccupied
until Grant pulled the pickup in.

They were a reminder the house was empty, as if he
needed one. That he alone was responsible for the health

and welfare of the tiny girl slumped against his side in sleep. And once again, that he was without a baby-sitter.

Frustration swept him, so sudden and strong that he wanted to slam a fist against the steering wheel. What did he have to do to find someone who wasn't more interested in him than his daughter? Instead of abusing the pickup, he pushed the automatic opener and listened to the door grumble to a close. Taking a deep breath, he gathered Cassie in his arms and made his way into the cool, silent house to her room.

He pulled blankets close up under her chin, then brushed a knuckle against her silken cheek. He had to find another baby-sitter, one who would fill their needs without wanting to occupy his bed. In the meantime, Cassie would keep on going to day care during the day. And he would continue to rely on Sharon for help.

Three days later, Grant learned he needed to go to Southern California for a week. He called on Sharon once again.

"Of course I will watch her," she immediately agreed.

"I'm sorry to have to be a bother—"

"Don't be silly, Grant. You needn't worry about me. It's Cassie you should be worried about." She paused, then quietly added, "You're spending too much time away from her."

"I have to go," he said, and wasn't sure whom he was trying to convince.

"I don't want you to."

Cassie's lower lip was thrust out, trembling, when he told her that evening. Pain squeezed his heart at the sight of tears shimmering in her eyes. "Hey," he said softly, drawing her to him with a hug. "You'll get to be with Sharon for a whole week. Plus your buddy Brittany. And I'll bring you something really special."

She brightened a little at that, but still cried when he dropped her off at Sharon's Sunday evening.

Guilt clung to him like a dark shroud as he flew from Valdez to Anchorage, then Seattle and on to Irvine. Guilt that once again he was asking Sharon for help, and once more he was leaving Cassie behind.

Yet his job as construction manager demanded it. This very job allowed him to provide Cassie with anything she needed and then some. He would give his daughter the world if he could, and if that demanded sacrifice, he would sacrifice.

A fact his father-in-law was quick to point out the following evening.

"We both know without question that you are trying, that you are doing the best you can for Cassie…under the circumstances." Hugh leaned into the restaurant table toward Grant, while the murmur of voices filled the air around them.

"I appreciate that," Grant answered as a prickle of apprehension raced along his spine. Perhaps it was the way that Hugh reached for Dorothy's hand, as if to reassure her or maybe gain support. Perhaps it was the way that Dorothy would not meet Grant's gaze, but instead nervously toyed with the linen napkin. Or maybe it was the unbidden memory of how they had pushed him away during Catherine's illness. Whatever, Grant suddenly wished he hadn't told them he was going to be in town for business. He should have dissuaded them from driving up from San Diego to meet him for dinner.

The conversation died, and silence held sway while the waiter cleared their dinner dishes and poured coffee. Then they had to talk, had to do something other than sit mutely, separated by far more than just a table.

Hugh drained his wineglass, cleared his throat. Then he

squared his thin shoulders and met Grant's gaze. "We were wondering if...thinking that maybe Cassie would be better off with us."

Grant arched a brow, choosing his words with care. "I appreciate the offer, but I think it's best that she stay home for a while, until we get better adjusted to the situation. Maybe this spring she can come and spend a few days."

"And how many baby-sitters will you have gone through by then? How many business trips?" Red slowly climbed Hugh's neck.

Grant stiffened. "I can't—"

"Son, we aren't suggesting that you don't love Cassie. We aren't suggesting she come for a visit, either."

He said the words so quietly that for a minute, Grant thought he'd heard wrong. Until Hugh continued.

"I think we can offer her a more stable home than you seem able to do."

Shock washed through Grant with a coldness that left him speechless. He could only stare at his father-in-law, and feel every ounce of blood drain from his face.

Then anger swept him, so overwhelming he gripped the edge of the table to force himself not to physically strike the man who sat before him. A man he had admired and thought of as being the father Grant had lost to a fishing vessel accident when he was a child. The man who had the nerve to suggest, for even a minute, that he give up Cassie.

He should have expected something like this after the way they'd acted while Catherine was ill, but he hadn't. He didn't dare release his hold on the table while he fought to remain silent, to remain seated until he had a semblance of control over the rage roaring through his veins.

Finally, he swallowed hard, then slowly stood until he towered above Hugh and Dorothy. He placed both hands flat on the tabletop and leaned slightly toward them. "Icicles will grow in Hell before anyone takes Cassie from me," he said quietly.

He turned and walked away without a backward glance.

By the end of the week, the bank lobby was a hub of activity. Customers rushed in to take care of last-minute business just prior to closing. Phones rang; voices rose in a murmur, punctuated by a shouted greeting or burst of laughter.

Sharon looked up from her office and watched with pleasure the swift efficiency with which the tellers handled the customers' needs. The past week had been good for business, Cassie a pleasure to have, and now Grant was home, a day early.

She frowned. Grant. She worried about him, about the effect his absences were having on Cassie. About—

The phone rang, jerking her from her thoughts. "Sharon speaking."

"Sharon, Grant here. Hey, I need a favor. I'm in the middle of a meeting and—"

"You're going to be late—could I pick Cassie up," Sharon quietly finished for him. "Grant, you just got back. Don't you think—"

"There is nothing I can do about it," he said. "Can you help me out?"

She sighed. "You know I can, but you owe Cassie, big-time. I'll take her to my place and bake cookies or something."

"Don't do dinner. I'll pick up pizza." He hung up.

"Pizza!" Sharon slapped the receiver down harder than necessary, glaring at it as if she could somehow conjure Grant in its place. She pushed back her anger, then stood and reached for her coat. Cassie was going to be disappointed.

Cassie was nowhere in sight when Sharon stepped into

the brightly lit room at day care. Jean Simon, the owner, walked over to greet her.

"Cassie is in the time-out room."

Sharon's heart sank. "That's the third time this week."

Jean nodded, mass of blond curls bouncing, as they turned toward a small hall. "I tried calling Grant, but he's been in meetings all day. This has been a bad week, although, to be honest, I almost prefer a Cassie with a temper to the silent little ghost she was for a while. Anything different going on at home?"

Other than an absentee father?

Sharon didn't say the words they were probably both thinking. Instead, she replied, "Not that I know of. What happened this time?"

"She got into a fight with Johnny Whitaker."

"He's twice her size!"

"Yeah, well." Jean shook her head with a small smile. "All I can say is, she's got a future in boxing if she wants it." They paused at the door. "She looks pretty bad, but if it helps, he's got two shiners. And his parents aren't going to cause any problems. I think they were both so embarrassed he got beaten up by a girl they would just as soon forget it happened." She swung the door open, then left.

Cassie sat in an orange plastic chair, shoulders hunched, head hung, legs slowly swinging.

"Cassie?" Sharon walked toward her. Cassie slowly raised her head, right eye nearly swollen shut, circled with black and blue, with a little green and purple thrown in. Sharon swallowed a gasp and forced herself not to rush forward, instead folding her arms across her chest.

"He called me a name," Cassie said, chin thrust out, good eye narrowing.

"And you couldn't have just ignored him?"

Silence answered the question they both knew wasn't really a question.

"Daddy working late tonight?" Cassie asked defiantly.

She looked small and defenseless. Pain pinched Sharon's heart.

"Yes," she answered, then opened her arms. "Come on over here for a hug."

Cassie hesitated a second, then slid from the chair. Sharon squeezed the little girl tight, wanting, wishing, aching. She swallowed the urge to scream. If Grant had been standing next to her, she would have choked him. Instead, she hugged tighter and said, "He's bringing pizza for dinner, so he shouldn't be too late."

An hour later the front door opened and Grant hollered, "Anyone home?"

Cassie rushed from the kitchen, Brittany bouncing at her heels, and Sharon was left to put the last of the cooling cookies away. She forced herself to slowly wash and dry her hands, and carefully compose her face before she turned and greeted Grant when she heard him walk into the kitchen. Cassie walked quietly at his side, clearly suffering from a scolding. Only the pup looked happy, eyes bright, whole body wiggling with excitement.

Sharon forced a smile. Grant met her gaze, then said, "Cassie, go wash up." He waited until the little girl was out of earshot. "Shall I lie down on the floor so you can stomp on me now?" His voice was quiet, tinged with weariness.

Sharon tried not to notice the dark shadows beneath his eyes, the hollows in his cheeks that had deepened since last week, the way he held himself so tensely, almost rigidly, though exhaustion clearly etched his face.

Anger fled as quickly as it had come. "Oh, sit down," she said quietly. "Stomping is too good for you. Besides, you know as well as I do that I never can stay mad at you. Even when you deserve it.''

A smile curved his lips but didn't erase the weariness in his eyes. He set the pizza on the table, walked to the fridge and pulled out a soda. Snapping the can open, he turned to face her. "I'm sorry I had to call you at the last minute like that.''

"So am I, but only for Cassie. You know I enjoy having her.''

He nodded, then tipped the can to take a long swallow of carbonated drink. Then he set the soda on the counter he now leaned against. "I don't mean to take advantage—''

"That should be the least of your worries,'' she said.

He paused. "I didn't know what else to do.''

"Maybe you should have bowed out of the meeting.''

"I couldn't.''

"And if I hadn't been able to pick Cassie up?''

He shoved his hands into his jeans pockets and didn't answer. He bowed his head slightly, and his dark-blue eyes suddenly filled with a bleakness that sent chills along Sharon's spine. He seemed so very alone.

She stepped closer, laid a hand against his chest in unspoken support. Grant lifted his head, dark gaze intense.

"That is one hell of a shiner she has.''

"I know.'' Sharon let her hand slide from him with a sigh and a step back. "I suppose we should be grateful she's coming out of her shell. But she was in trouble three times this week.'' She took a deep breath, then plunged on, certain he wouldn't want to hear her words but believing a lesser friend would keep silent.

"Grant, I know you are doing your best, but Cassie needs more of your time.'' She ignored the tightening of his mouth, the narrowing of his eyes. "You work too many long hours, and...well...I wonder if you understand how hard it is for her when you're gone. And I can't help but wonder how much longer you can do this alone, Grant. I am not—''

"I can't believe I'm hearing this," Grant said in a low, hard voice.

Anger blazed in his eyes. Sharon automatically took a half step back at the intensity.

"First Catherine's parents and now you. Well, you are wrong. Damned wrong." He swept a hand through his hair, leaving it tousled. "I cannot believe that you are even saying this. I *thought* we were friends."

His eyes were glittering, accusing her of betrayal. Sharon mentally stiffened, then lifted her chin and met his gaze without flinching. "You know very well we're friends, but that has nothing to do with the subject at hand."

He arched a brow, a dark slash that seemed to accentuate the anger she sensed simmering inside him.

"What exactly are you suggesting I do? If you think for one minute that I am going to hand my daughter over to my in-laws, think again." His voice turned acidic.

"I have no answers," she snapped, stung by the tone of his voice. "Nor am I suggesting anything of the kind. All I am saying is that the present situation is not good enough. Okay? Not for you. Not for Cassie."

Silence stretched between them, fraught with tension.

"I love my daughter. I wouldn't do anything to hurt her," Grant finally said.

The huskiness in his voice tugged at Sharon's heart. She swallowed a sudden lump in her throat and ached for both Cassie and Grant. "I know you do," she half whispered, "and so do I." Then she cleared her throat. "I am sorry I brought it up. It's just…well…it is important. I'm worried about Cassie. And I'm worried about you."

Grant tucked Cassie into bed, wincing each time he looked at the black eye. It didn't take an intellectual giant to see that her temper had worsened since Catherine's death and that his absences did not help, but what was he to do? His job required a lot of his time. It also provided them with a nice home, and Cassie a closet full of clothes and an overflowing toy box.

He remembered well the sharp-edged knife of need, of want, when others had seemed to have it all and he had nothing. The humiliation of wearing secondhand jeans, owning two pairs of socks and one pair of shoes—the cheapest sneakers to be had—when starting grade school. His hands tightened into fists. Cassie would never suffer that sort of humiliation. Ever.

His mother had done her best, but being widowed and left with three boys to raise had not been easy. He had started mowing lawns and shoveling sidewalks to earn money when he was nine, and had been working ever since.

He shuddered, forced his fists to relax and shook off the memory before it dragged him deeper into the past. After closing Cassie's bedroom door, he walked to the den, flipped on the desk light and settled into the leather chair.

Sharon's words haunted him. He knew she'd spoken from the heart with the best of intentions, and that she'd spoken from experience. As a child of parents who were commercial fishermen, Sharon had suffered violent motion sickness on even the calmest of days at sea, so each fishing season she had lived with Grant and his family. She knew well what it was like to be left by her family for long periods of time. Which was exactly why Grant could not dismiss her words easily.

If only his mother lived closer than Seattle, if she were in better health.... He mentally snorted. If only...what a waste of time!

Both brothers lived in the lower forty-eight, thousands of miles from being any help. They had their own families, their own lives. And he knew with chilling certainty that Cassie did not need another sitter. She needed a mother.

A mother could not be had without that woman first becoming his wife.

Wife. He closed his eyes and fought the memories. But the night seemed ripe for ghosts of the past, so they came, stronger than he this time, whirling through his mind with a flood of muted color like old photographs, faded, corners curled.

Catherine, face flushed with happiness on their wedding day. Happier yet with the birth of Cassie. A fleeting happiness soon dimmed, replaced by a growing anger and discontentment. She had hated Anchorage and wanted to move back to California, though she had known before their marriage he had every intention of living in Alaska and building a career there. Grant had hoped, as a last straw, that accepting a promotion to construction manager and moving to Valdez, building a new house, would please her, would somehow provide the miracle needed to salvage their marriage. But it hadn't. She had immediately hated Valdez, almost as much as she did Grant for bringing her there, and was preparing to take Cassie to California and divorce him, when she suddenly fell ill.

He had tried everything he could think of to make her happy and had failed. Nothing seemed able to prevent the downward spiral, the disintegration of their marriage, except illness. Cancer. Frightened, angry and blaming, Catherine had clung to him, though their love had long died. He'd held and soothed her, accepted the blame and watched, totally helpless as death relentlessly claimed her with a swiftness that allowed little time for forgiveness.

Cold washed through him. He sprang to his feet, heart pounding, hands clenched. Sweat dampened the back of his shirt. He snapped the lamp off and strode down the hall to his room.

He would never put himself in such a vulnerable position again. Any love he had left was for Cassie, and Cassie alone.

The last thing he wanted was another wife.

Chapter Two

Three women answered his ad for an in-home baby-sitter.

Marcie, with long, blond hair hanging straight down her back. Black, shiny tights topped by a low-cut blouse showing far more than a hint of cleavage left nothing to the imagination. She had a disconcerting habit of leaning toward Grant, which he supposed was designed to raise his blood pressure. It did—not with lust but with anger. When she suggested it would be best for all if she moved in with them, he concluded the interview and walked her to the door, not bothering to have her meet Cassie.

A dull throb began in his brow.

Sandra was a quiet woman, with pale-gray eyes that seemed to match her spirit. She was in the process of going through a divorce and wasn't sure how long she would remain in Valdez. It depended, she said, on whether she met another man soon, because she was not a woman who could live without a man in her life. Grant thanked her for coming, ushered her from the house without meeting Cassie and crossed his fingers that the next woman would be perfect.

The throb turned to a pounding.

Beth had six children, watched five others and needed to earn more money because her good-for-nothing ex-husband was behind on child support once more. Though Grant felt the full impact of her imploring eyes, he thanked her, also, and explained that he would keep her in mind if he couldn't find someone who would come to his home to care for Cassie. Cassie remained in her room, playing.

The pounding exploded into a full-blown headache that had him pinching the bridge of his nose as he settled back into the leather chair in the den.

"Did you find one?" Cassie asked from the doorway.

Grant shook his head as she crossed the room and crawled onto his lap. She tucked her head beneath his chin and the headache began to dim.

"Maybe Sharon would do it," Cassie said in a small voice.

"Honey, Sharon has a job, remember? How would they run the bank without her?" Sharon would be perfect, he thought, tightening his arms slightly.

"Oh."

Silence.

"I wish Mama didn't die."

Her voice was but a sad murmur that drove nails of guilt into his heart. "I know you do, pumpkin. So do I," he finally answered in a harsh whisper. Then he squeezed her in a tight hug, as if able to protect her from all pain, past and future—an impossible task that made it all the more important.

They sat in silence in the heavy dusk of the room. Snow fell from gray clouds; thick, fat flakes captured in the frame of the window. Cassie snuggled closer to Grant. He held her close, heart aching with love, and wondered what he was going to do.

* * *

Grant's anger filled Sharon's kitchen in almost visible waves. He stormed from counter to counter, jaw clenched so tight she feared for his teeth. She was thankful that Cassie was playing with Brittany in the backyard, enjoying the six inches of new snow.

He turned and slapped Hugh's letter on the table with a thump. "I can't believe Hugh and Dorothy, that they have the nerve…" He swallowed as if to gain control. "I simply cannot believe they are doing this to me, to Cassie, after all that we've been through." He ground the words through clenched teeth.

"Read it—read the damned thing." He nearly flung the letter at her.

Sharon shook her head and pushed it away. "It's not my letter to read," she said. "Besides, I think you told me everything they said."

"You're right."

He sighed, ran a hand through his hair, then slumped into a chair opposite her. Dark circles shadowed his glittering eyes. Sharon wished with all her heart that something she could do or say would change matters.

He leaned toward her, eyes burning. "Don't they understand I am trying…trying to find a damned sitter. And I don't ask to go on business trips. I shouldn't have to travel so much once the project starts, just a few more months." He closed his eyes briefly.

Sharon reached to clasp his large hand, which was clenched in a tight fist. He brought his gaze to hers and held it.

"They think they can provide a better, more stable home for Cassie. A better home for my daughter than I can provide." A muscle leaped in his jaw, then tightened.

Her heart ached for her friend. "I know you don't want to hear this, Grant, but though misguided, they mean well,'' she said softly. "They aren't suggesting a change in custody to hurt you.''

He pulled his hand away to drum his fingers against the table, frowning.

"They love Cassie and only want what's best for her,'' she added.

"And taking her from her father is best?'' He nearly spit the words.

Sharon shook her head. "No, I don't think so, but—''

Grant held a hand to stop her. "They want what can't be had—their daughter back. And since that won't happen, they want mine.'' His voice grew harder as he spoke. "I'm not even sure having a sitter would matter. They would probably question the permanence. The only way to provide a foolproof solution—'' he emphasized the words "—is for me to marry. And it will be a cold day in hell before that happens.''

"Grant, you won't always feel that way. With time—''

"Time? To hell with time. To hell with Hugh and Dorothy. They want Cassie as replacement for Catherine, as payment because I took her from them and brought her back in a coffin.''

"No.'' Sharon nearly shouted the word, frustrated and a little angry herself. Grant arched a brow. She continued, shaking her head. "You're twisting this, distorting it, Grant. Hugh and Dorothy are not vindictive people—''

"Aren't they? You weren't there, didn't see how they acted toward the end,'' he shot back with an angry growl.

"Maybe they did act a little strange, but that is certainly understandable under the circumstances.'' She paused. "You might have read more into it than was meant.'' He snorted. She ignored him and continued. "There is no way I can really know, but I don't think they are doing this to make life hard for you. If they're guilty of anything, it's of loving Cassie, and we are all guilty of that.''

"Are you defending them?" He glared at her.

"Only their right to care." She glared back.

"You need to keep in mind that this is not about you or me or Hugh and Dorothy," she finally said quietly. "It's about Cassie and what is best for her."

After a minute of silence, Grant dropped his gaze. He carefully folded the rumpled letter and slid it into his pocket. Then he looked at her. "I am sorry for losing my temper like that. It wasn't fair to you," he said quietly.

She reached out to cover his hand with hers again. A large hand that dwarfed hers in comparison. "Don't be silly, Grant. We're friends, and that's all part of what friends are for. To be there to listen. You would do the same for me."

He didn't answer. Didn't move a muscle.

"Maybe you should consider letting me care for Cassie on a permanent basis in the evenings when you're gone. It might ease Hugh and Dorothy's concerns. They've met me and know I love her. I'm certainly stable, don't plan to be moving anywhere, and I'm not looking for marriage." She paused. He remained silent. "I won't meet you at the door in anything sexier than a pair of sweats," she added. "I promise."

Grant half smiled, suddenly looking tired by the effort, then withdrew his hand to run it through his hair. "No. I won't let you do that. This is my problem. I'll solve it."

"You can't always—"

"Sharon." Grant reached to cover her hands with his. A brief, friendly clasp. "You do far more for me than anyone can expect and I appreciate it. But I cannot allow you to take on the two of us on a permanent basis."

She opened her mouth to argue, to say that she wanted to.

"No," he said firmly.

And she knew he meant it.

* * *

Grant had to go to Anchorage for meetings, just over-night, but Cassie clung to him at the airport and sobbed as if she would never see him again.

"I have to go, Cass. You know that. I'll be back to-morrow, I promise," Grant repeated over and over again as he held his daughter.

His eyes glittered when they met Sharon's, and he looked as if his heart were being ripped out. She felt as though hers was.

She reached to touch his arm. "She'll be okay once you're gone," she said.

His eyes held her for one long minute. "I wouldn't leave her if I didn't know that. And there's no one I trust my daughter with more than you," he said in a husky voice.

A sudden lump in Sharon's throat prevented an answer. She silently squeezed Grant's arm, then stepped back.

"I have got to go, Cass. The plane is getting ready to leave," Grant whispered, and pressed one last kiss to her brow. His hands trembled as he handed the small girl to Sharon. Cassie wound her arms around Sharon's neck, bur-ied her face in her shoulder and sobbed.

"Goodbye," Sharon murmured, and held Cassie's trem-bling body as Grant strode out to the plane. She cajoled Cassie into watching as the plane lumbered across the run-way, to turn and race forward, before finally climbing into the sky with a great roar. Cassie's sobs quit, her tears dry-ing on her cheeks.

"Shall we go home and see what Brittany is doing?" Sharon asked.

Cassie nodded, then wiggled to be released. She slipped a small hand into Sharon's hand. A hand that gripped Sharon's heart, as well.

And there's no one I trust my daughter with more than you.

Warmth washed through her, as she remembered

Grant's husky words. His trust, his friendship, was as precious a gift as Cassie's love.

She glanced down at the top of Cassie's head, at the slightly crooked part in the shiny black hair and the butterfly-shaped barrette at the top of each braid, and her heart swelled. She loved Cassie so much it sometimes frightened her. What was she going to do when Grant did remarry one day? And she had little doubt that eventually he would. A man with his looks, his resources. It wouldn't…hadn't taken long for women to notice. It was only a matter of time until Grant reciprocated the interest.

Would a new wife welcome or allow their friendship to continue? Would there be room for her in their lives?

She doubted it. And the thought of not having Cassie and Grant as part of her life was almost too painful to bear.

Grant met with an attorney while in Anchorage. The attorney confirmed that although there was always a chance he could lose Cassie, it was highly unlikely. At most, this challenge to his custody of Cassie would probably be an expensive inconvenience, something to worry at him like a splinter. With time it would go away. He advised Grant to talk to Hugh and Dorothy and come up with some way to set their minds at ease and avoid an unnecessary legal battle.

Hell, if he could do that, there wouldn't be a problem.

A knot of tension tied itself permanently in his gut. He snapped at his secretary, apologized, then snapped again. He made a list of his options, crossed things off, added them again, only to cross them off once more. Sitters. Nannies. A wife.

Sitters, not permanent. Nannies, unavailable in Valdez, and not permanent. And even if he found one in Anchorage, how long would she be happy living in Valdez, isolated by surrounding wilderness and sea?

He toyed with the idea of taking Sharon up on her offer, of hiring her to watch Cassie in the evenings while he was away. But...not only was that unfair to Sharon, it was not a permanent solution. Sharon had her own life to live, and one day she would marry and want a family of her own, and where would that leave them? Generous though her offer was, he could not accept it on a long-term basis.

The last option was a wife.

But he simply did not have the emotional resources to deal with a wife. The very thought sent chills along his spine.

The next day a letter from an attorney came express mail, an official demand for custody of Cassie from his in-laws. Grant opened the letter late evening, after Cassie was in bed.

Anger rose in him as he read, then fear. Even the tiniest of chances that he could lose Cassie overwhelmed him. And the sense of betrayal, of attack, from people he loved was incredibly painful. As well, he did not want to alienate Hugh and Dorothy, because Cassie loved her grandparents and they her. They had all suffered a tremendous loss and didn't need to lose one another, as well.

A whirlwind of conflicting thoughts and emotions spun in his head. Like a vortex of vibrant colors that did nothing more than whirl and spin and slam up against black solid walls of no answers.

The room seemed to shrink. He was suffocating. Choking. He fought the feeling, resisted it with every fiber of his being, until he finally had to rush through the house to the deck. Bitter cold greeted him; frozen fingers of winter gripped his bare skin. Biting, burning his lungs as he drew deep breaths to steady himself. He felt unable to ease the feeling of impending doom.

The phone rang, jerking him back into the house. Grant stiffened at the sound of Hugh's voice, and he fought the urge either to slam the phone down or to unload the emotional turmoil that still churned in his gut.

"How about letting Cassie come stay with us for a while?" Hugh offered.

"You want custody of my daughter because I'm gone too much, yet you're suggesting I send her down there, where I'll hardly ever see her, for who knows how long? That makes a lot of sense."

"And you going off and leaving her with a baby-sitter, a different one every few months is good?" Hugh's voice rose.

"She's my daughter, Hugh. Do you think I would do anything to harm her?" He took a deep breath. "You don't have the right to do this, to hurt us more than we already have been. Cassie is my daughter. She belongs with me." His voice was low, hard. His heart pounded painfully in his chest.

"If you couldn't keep a wife happy, what makes you think you can be a good parent?" Hugh cried.

"It's time for this conversation to end, before we both say things we will only regret," Grant answered quietly, suppressed anger knotting in his throat.

Hugh paused. "This isn't about you or me, Grant. It's about what is best for Cassie."

"Is it?" Grant asked softly with a thread of steel in his voice. "Catherine is gone, Hugh. Cassie is not going to replace her. And until you decide to drop this lawsuit, we have nothing to discuss."

His hand trembled when he hung up. He shut his eyes for one long minute, half expecting the phone to ring again, then slowly walked over to the window when it didn't. The lights of the town burned below, throwing shadows on the snow that spread across lawns and roofs, so that it looked like a thick layer of winter butter.

If you couldn't keep a wife happy, what makes you think you can be a good parent?

Hugh's words returned. Unbidden. Unwanted.

Pain slammed through Grant, taking his breath away. His hands curled into fists as a wave of guilt followed. As the memory of Catherine's unhappiness unrolled in his mind.

He'd tried. Oh, how he had tried.

And he had failed.

The words screamed through his mind, angry accusations from the past.

Head bowed, fists clenched, he fought the memory. What happened between he and Catherine had nothing— not one damned thing—to do with his being a good parent to Cassie. He slowly raised his head. Forced each finger to unfurl.

The only thing that mattered was what was best for Cassie.

That is all he wanted and worked so hard for. It would be easier if he could deny his absences did not have much impact on Cassie, but he couldn't. The walls inched closer once again.

It would be easier if he could deny that Hugh's concerns had some validity. He couldn't.

Regardless, he would never give Cassie up. To anyone. He couldn't quit his job—he had to work to be able to provide for his daughter. Baby-sitters and nannies weren't the answer. He took a deep breath, then another and a third, as his mind circled the truth like a wary wolf a trap.

He needed to find a mother for Cassie. A wife.

As soon as possible.

The very thought chilled his soul.

* * *

"I have decided to get married," Grant told Sharon the next evening over fresh-baked pie and coffee in her kitchen.

"Married?" she echoed, color draining from her face.

The darkness of her eyes, filled with shock, pulled at him. The shiny mass of dark red-brown curls that stopped at the curve of jaw made her skin seem even paler. Skin that would be soft to the touch.

He frowned and looked away.

A shout of laughter, the bark of a dog, drifted through the window from the backyard. Cassie was playing out back with Brittany.

"I didn't know you were seeing anyone," Sharon finally said.

"I'm not." Grant shoved his empty plate back, forced himself to look at her. "I am thinking...planning to run an ad in the Anchorage paper."

Her mouth dropped open, then she snapped it shut. "You've given up on finding a sitter," she said flatly.

"Not permanent enough."

"I see." She slowly pushed her plate back. "Are you that worried about losing Cassie? I thought the attorney said—"

"It's not just the custody suit. Cassie needs a mother and there is only one way I know to provide that," he said grimly. "You yourself suggested I do something."

"I suggested that you spend more time with your daughter," she said quietly. "And I also offered to watch Cassie for you."

"Sharon, you know that I appreciate everything you do, everything that you have done for Cassie, but I need to find a permanent solution. And I can't accept your offer. It wouldn't be fair to you."

After a minute, she cleared her throat. "Why an ad, Grant? Why not marry someone you know, someone who

cares at least a little about Cassie?" She continued before
he could speak. "Maybe you should do something tem-
porary. Let me watch her the way I offered and start dat-
ing. In time you'll get over losing Catherine, Grant, and
meet someone you can love again."

Grant laughed, a harsh, humorless burst of sound. "If it
wasn't for Cassie, I would never marry again." He slowly
enunciated each cold word.

Sharon's eyes widened. She opened her mouth as if to
argue, then closed it.

He chose his words carefully. "This is going to be a
business deal only, with a contract up front, a salary and
a bonus for completion."

Sharon slowly shook her head.

"It's no different from hiring a sitter or a nanny," he
argued. "You know as well as I that if I hired a live-in,
half the town would have us involved or at least in bed
with each other unless she was ninety-five and in a wheel-
chair, and maybe even then. At least if I contract someone
for marriage, she'll know up front exactly what I expect.
There will be no emotional involvement or expectation
between us. And no one, not Hugh or Dorothy or anyone
else, can find fault with the situation."

"You can't pay someone to love Cassie," she said quietly.

"I would hope they would come to love her." He
sighed, suddenly tired. "I have to do this, Sharon. It's not
a perfect solution, a perfect world, but there isn't a thing
I can do about that."

Sharon tossed and turned, squeezed her eyes shut, tried
to force sleep—and finally gave up. The digital letters on
the clock confirmed that it was four in the morning. Brittany burrowed deeper on the blankets and watched with

sleepy eyes as Sharon pulled on a pair of worn sweats. At least it was Saturday, so she could nap later.

The thoughts that had haunted her throughout the night returned full force. Grant was going to marry. She closed her eyes briefly. Brittany trotted at her heels as Sharon headed for the kitchen, badly in need of a cup of coffee. Cold air greeted her as she shooed the sleepy pup out into the backyard, then turned toward the coffeepot.

I have decided to get married.

The words seemed to shriek through her mind, through the silence of the winter's early morning, as a layer of dark quiet and frigid temperatures covered Alaska like a thick, impenetrable quilt. Exhausted from a sleepless night, she told herself for about the ten-millionth time that she was overreacting. The coffeepot choked and gargled. Brittany barked, then shook snow from herself when Sharon let her in.

It's not a perfect solution, a perfect world, but there isn't a thing I can do about that.

Although she well knew that, Grant's words still caused her heart to ache. In a perfect world she would not have gotten the infection that had hospitalized her just months after getting married, then had kept her flat on her back in bed for three weeks at home, leaving her so badly scarred internally that she was unable to give her husband the children they both so desperately wanted. In a perfect world Charley would not have stopped loving her because of it, would not have left her for a pregnant girlfriend who happened to be Sharon's best friend. Catherine wouldn't have gotten ill. The list could go on.

She poured a cup of coffee, wandered into the living room to pull the drapes, then curled on the love seat to watch as snow drifted to the ground. Brittany curled next to her, chin resting on Sharon's ankle.

In a perfect world, she would have been pretty enough

to catch Grant's interest and they would have fallen in love. Instead, she'd had to endure their high school years, watching Grant date the prettiest girls while she went unnoticed. By college, she had reconciled herself to the fact that she and Grant would be nothing more than friends. Yet when he had brought Catherine home to meet the family, then married the sophisticated, beautiful blonde, Sharon had been shattered with a sense of loss.

And now he was doing it to her again. Marrying another woman.

Why not me? The thought welled up from within, so strong and unexpected that Sharon nearly sputtered taking a sip of coffee.

Don't be ridiculous, she told herself. She was not feeling sorry for herself, but unless something miraculous happened to her overnight, Grant would be no more interested in marrying her than he would a—

She put the coffee cup on the end table with shaking hands.

Grant was going to marry a stranger, without emotional commitment. Why wouldn't he marry her?

Why would she want him to?

Cassie. The answer whispered through her mind with a sense of rightness. In fact, the more she thought about it, the more it made sense. She wasn't asking for an emotional commitment. By marrying Grant, she would become a mother to a little girl she loved dearly.

Mother. She closed her eyes at the rush of emotion that simple word brought. Something she had always wanted and would never have. It wouldn't matter that she couldn't have children, because intimacy would not be part of the bargain.

And she would not lose Grant again.

You have lost your marbles, she told herself sternly.

And then began planning what she was going to say to convince Grant that she hadn't.

By the time the sun finally filtered thin light through the clouds, the coffeepot was drained and Sharon had nearly paced a path in the living room carpet. She glared at the clock as if it were a mortal enemy, paced some more, then glared at the clock again.

When it struck ten, she gathered courage and reached for the phone to dial Grant's number with trembling fingers. A quick trip to the store for muffins, and fifteen minutes later she and Brittany pulled into Grant's snow-blown driveway.

Cassie met them at the door, bundled in brilliant-red snow pants and jacket. "Daddy said I could play outside with Brittany. Is that okay? Please, Sharon?" Her eyes pleaded unnecessarily.

"Keep her leash on, and look out for cars." Sharon paused to watch as the little girl clambered up the snow-bank and into the empty lot next door, Brittany bouncing at her side. The two were vivid splashes of color in motion against blinding white.

She turned, entered the house and slowly closed the door. She swallowed hard, fighting a sudden urge to spin around and run as fast as she could before it was too late.

"In here," Grant shouted from the kitchen.

"Coffee?" he offered as she entered the brightly lit room.

"Milk would be better," she answered. She lifted the bag she carried. "Muffin? I got poppy seed."

He grinned. Her pulse leaped.

Nerves, she told herself as she shrugged out of her jacket and settled at the table. A minute later, Grant sank into a chair opposite, steam rising from the dark, rich liquid in his cup, golden muffins on a plate between them.

"So," he said after a large swallow of coffee. "What did you need to talk about?"

Whiskers shadowed his lean jaw, and his eyes captured and held her as though she were under a spell. Her throat dried. She opened her mouth to speak, but couldn't find the breath to push words out. Could not find the words, period.

"You okay?" Grant arched a brow.

Heat flooded her face. She quickly nodded, grabbed her glass of milk as if it were a lifeline and took a swallow. Carefully setting the glass aside, she took a deep breath as Grant lifted his cup.

"I am answering your ad," she said.

He sputtered, spilling coffee down the front of his T-shirt. Sharon gasped. Grant sprang to his feet, ripped off the shirt and grabbed a dish towel. He mopped the front of his chest and glared at her.

One look at his broad, well-muscled chest covered with thick, black curly hair and Sharon jerked her gaze to his face and kept it there, heart and pulse racing.

"My ad?" he asked softly.

She lifted her chin slightly and tried to still her pounding pulse and heart. "Yes, your ad. I think we should get married."

He froze, dropping the towel to his side.

They stared at each other, gazes locked. Grant's eyes were without a trace of expression. Sharon was filled with shock that she'd actually said the words. But now that they were out her resolve strengthened, even as she mentally cringed from his reaction.

"Why in the hell would you want to marry me?" His words were carefully enunciated. His eyes wary. He dropped into his chair.

"You can quit looking as if you think I am going to leap across the table and try to have my way with you.

I'm not one of your past baby-sitters," she said, heat filling her cheeks. "It's not you I want...I mean...not in that way...it's Cassie. I love Cassie and I don't want to lose her, and regardless of what you say, if you marry someone I will lose her. I don't think I could bear that, Grant."

"Aren't you over—"

"No," she cried, suddenly impatient.

"Let me get this straight. You love Cassie so much that you'll enter a loveless marriage with me? Are you listening to yourself, Sharon? That is nuts!"

Sharon lifted her chin a notch, eyes narrowing. "Says the man who is planning to marry a total stranger. One he's going to advertise for in the paper and purchase. Grant, finding a wife isn't like getting a puppy."

He flushed as his jaw tensed. "I wasn't planning on using the pet section. And I thought I made it perfectly clear that I'm doing this for Cassie."

"Well, so am I. Is it so hard to believe I could love your daughter as much as you? Think about it—"

"No." He shook his head emphatically.

"Why not?" She balled her hands.

"Because you should be marrying some guy you love and having children of your own—that's why. You've always wanted a large family." Grant bit out the words. "I have nothing to offer you—"

"Except Cassie, a little girl I already love as if she were my own." Sharon took a deep breath to calm her racing emotions. "I'm not asking you for more than that Grant." She paused, then added quietly, "I'm not asking for your love, only your friendship."

Grant just stared at her. She swallowed hard, then continued. "After Charley left me, I swore I would never marry again."

"You'll change your mind in time," he said in a low voice.

"No, I won't, and you have no right assuming you know my mind better than I do. I haven't accepted a date since the divorce, and that's been a few years. As hard as it may be to believe, it's not as though I haven't been asked, as if I haven't been offered opportunities."

"Of course you have," he said quietly.

She leaned toward Grant as if leaning against the tide, not certain it would make a difference but hoping to shorten the distance between them. "My only regret with my decision is that I don't have a family."

She almost told him more, but stopped. The last thing she wanted was Grant agreeing to marry her out of pity. Poor Sharon, who can't have children. She couldn't bear that.

Grant remained silent, frowning slightly.

"This is my opportunity to have that family," she added quietly.

He shook his head.

"Please think about it," she urged. "I know you don't want any emotional involvement, so why can't you believe that I would feel the same way? Grant, can you truly say that Cassie would be better off if you married a total stranger rather than someone she already knows and loves? Someone who loves her as much as I do?"

His dark eyes probed her as if trying to see into her mind. Her heart. She prayed he would give the idea a chance.

"It's no great secret that I care for you very much, but only as a friend. I'm not carrying a torch of unrequited love, if that's what you're worried about," Sharon added, quickly trying to second-guess any argument he might have. Honesty prompted her to add, "I know you were thinking about a full-time mother, but I would want to continue to work. Cassie could go to day care during the day. She needs to be with kids her own age, and she enjoys the other children, when she isn't fighting with them.''

Grant half smiled. Hope blossomed in Sharon's heart.

She pressed on, willing him to listen, to understand and to concede. ''I think if you give this some thought, you will see that it makes perfect sense. We have been friends forever and we still get along, something lots of married folks can't say. Neither of us wants to be married, but both of us wants the best for Cassie. You want a mother and I want a daughter.'' She paused, then said softly, ''It sounds like the perfect solution to me.''

Grant sat alone in the family room. A log cracked in the fireplace—a loud, popping noise—as flames licked along its side, fueled by bright orange coals beneath. The house settled a bit with a groan, not unlike an old man whose bones protested as he burrowed a little deeper beneath the covers. Except the house settled under a blanket of snow that had fallen steadily throughout the day and was only now starting to slacken.

All around him was darkness, except for the dancing, flickering light from the fire, which cast an orange-yellow glow that didn't quite penetrate the shadows. The clock on the mantel chimed twelve times with a solid certainty that Grant suddenly envied. Cassie had long since been tucked into bed, lost to the land of sleep and dreams. A land Grant wouldn't mind visiting himself...if only he could.

It sounds like the perfect solution to me.

Sharon's words haunted him, as they had since she'd uttered them, before she'd calmly walked from his kitchen to allow him to think about her offer.

He shouldn't need to think, should be able to dismiss the proposal as if it had never been spoken. But he couldn't. Arguments piled in his mind like the snow out-side, and remained there because he could not refute the truth. If he viewed the situation coldly and objectively, her proposal did sound like the perfect solution.

If Sharon truly meant that she didn't want to marry for love, did not want any emotional involvement. And he had no reason to think she was lying. She had always been honest with him in the past.

Why, then, would she want to marry him? She was far too young and attractive, warmhearted and giving, to tie herself to a man who would never offer her children of her own, never offer her a true marriage. A man who was not capable of loving again.

And yet, she knew that love and a houseful of children weren't being offered. That it would not be a marriage of the heart, and she still insisted it was what she wanted. Perhaps she had never gotten over the devastation of her divorce. His stomach tightened at the thought.

Did her reasons really matter?

He didn't want to marry Sharon. She was his friend, and a more honorable man would gently tell her no. Tell her that she deserved far better than the type of marriage he was offering, Charley and the past be damned.

Hell, he didn't want to marry anyone.

This isn't about you or me. It's about what is best for Cassie.

Hugh's words came to mind. It *was* about what was best for Cassie, his tiny daughter, whom he loved more than life itself. He cursed himself, because a stronger man would not even consider Sharon's offer.

Lord help him, he did not have the strength to walk away. He was going to marry Sharon, and hope they didn't live to regret it.

Chapter Three

Grant called Hugh the next morning. "You can drop the custody suit. I am getting married," he said.

"Married? But... I mean... To whom?" Hugh sputtered the words.

"Sharon O'Reily. You've met her."

"Of course...." Hugh's words died. Silence followed. "Don't do this, Grant. Don't do this to yourself or Cassie," he finally said, breathless, words clipped.

Grant arched his brow. He started to speak, but Hugh cut him off.

"It's too soon. You're rushing into this too quickly. You need time, more time. I can't—"

"And what about what's best for Cassie?" Grant asked coldly. "You're threatening to take her from me because I can't handle things alone. And now..." He swallowed his words, swallowed hard to slow the anger that threatened to explode. "It might interest you to know that my mother and Sharon's parents are delighted. They don't seem to share your concerns."

"We didn't want to drive you into a marriage," Hugh said as if Grant had not spoken. "Good grief, man, stop and think about what you're doing. I mean, Sharon seems a nice young woman, but do you really want to marry her? Is she—"

"She is the finest person I know." Grant slowly enunciated his words as he defended Sharon. His barely controlled anger turned to fury at the thought that Hugh would dare question Sharon's integrity.

"Of course she is, but—"

"We're getting married, Hugh. There isn't a thing that you and Dorothy can do or say to stop us, so you had better get used to the fact." He hung up the phone.

Nerves twisted a knot in Sharon's stomach on the drive over to Grant's. He'd not given her an answer when he called, just quietly asked if she could come over and talk.

What if he said no? The knot in her stomach tightened further at the thought. What if he said yes? Another twist in the knot. How would it affect their friendship?

Stop, she silently cried. These were questions she simply did not have answers for.

She pulled into the driveway, switched off the engine and just sat for a minute, listening to the creak and groan of the cooling engine, telling herself that everything would be fine. That no matter what happened, she and Grant would remain friends. And hoping that she was right.

Cassie met her at the front door, reaching for a hug from Sharon while trying to hug a wiggling Brittany at the same time. Sharon knelt so that the impossible could be accomplished.

"Why don't you take Brittany down to your room to play, Cass?"

Grant's low voice startled Sharon. She stood to face

him. He avoided her gaze, causing her nerves to tighten
further.

"But, Daddy, I wanta see Sharon." Cassie's voice took
on a whiny tone. "I wanta—"

"You can see Sharon later, after she and I have talked."
Grant answered patiently.

Cassie pouted and frowned but did as she was told,
dragging her feet, a tail-wagging Brittany at her side.

Grant turned to Sharon. "Would you like a cup of coffee?"

She didn't really, but nodded anyway, then walked by
his side into the kitchen. She sat at the table while he
silently filled two mugs, then joined her. Steam rose off
the dark liquid in a twisting mist. Grant still avoided her
gaze as he took a long swallow, then another. She gripped
her mug, fought the urge to yank his away, to force him
to speak. Awkward silence stretched between them, pulling
Sharon's nerves taut, tauter, until she felt they would snap.

He was going to turn her down. The longer the silence
stretched, the more certain she grew. Her spirits sank at
the thought.

"I accept your proposal," Grant said quietly.

Sharon's heart jerked in her chest and she barely kept
her mouth from dropping open. With dark, somber eyes,
he finally met her gaze.

"I think you're nuts for wanting to do this, but, viewed
selfishly, it's the perfect solution for me."

"You're not being selfish—"

"I am," he said firmly. "And once again you're rushing
to the rescue. Sharon—" he leaned closer, voice dropping
an octave "—this is not the same as staying up until two
in the morning typing my high school term paper because
I waited until the last minute to write it and couldn't type
it myself. And this is not the same as sharing the blame
with me when I caught the shed on fire trying to roast you

some hot dogs." He paused. "Why are you doing this, Sharon? We're talking a serious commitment here. You're going to be giving up a lot," he said in a husky voice.

"I am well aware of the seriousness of what I'm suggesting, Grant. I want to do this because I love Cassie with all my heart. And I care for you. You're the best friend I've ever had or ever will have, Grant." She could have added that it was because she wanted to be a mother so bad she ached. Added that she would never have children of her own. But the words stuck in her throat. She could not bear the pity, bear the chance that he would see her as flawed, less a person. Could not take the risk that she would somehow lose Grant if he knew.

"I don't understand your decision, but it's yours to make." Grant bowed his head, rubbing his brow with one hand. "We'll have separate bedrooms, of course. I don't think either of us is interested in the, ah...physical aspects of marriage." His voice was low.

She flushed. For a heartbeat, her pride cried out in wounded protest. *Idiot*, she told herself, *separate bedrooms* are *what you want*. She was marrying Grant to gain a daughter, not a bedmate. "Of course," she said. The heat in her cheeks began to recede.

"Are you absolutely certain you want to do this?" Grant's eyes captured her.

"Yes," she answered quietly in a steady voice.

He gave her a crooked smile that pulled at her heart.

"We'd better tell Cassie."

Cassie perched on Grant's lap, eyes wide and rounded like a small, startled owl, gaze firmly fixed on Sharon. Sharon battled disappointment even as Grant nudged Cassie. "Did you hear what I said?" he asked.

Cassie solemnly nodded. "Sharon is gonna live with us and be my mama," she said quietly.

Thick silence wrapped around them, quickly becoming uncomfortable. Grant arched a brow Sharon's way. She shrugged slightly, then focused on Cassie. "We thought that you would be happy I was coming to live with you."

Cassie hesitated, then silently nodded.

Sharon sat back, at a loss. While she may not have expected unbridled ecstasy, she had anticipated a far more positive reception than she was getting. Brittany snorted in her sleep, curled at Sharon's feet.

"Why don't you go on and play?" Grant urged. He quietly watched while Cassie slipped from his lap and disappeared around the corner of the den, Brittany jumping up, trotting after. He turned his gaze back to Sharon with a frown. "I don't get it. She's nuts about you."

"Maybe this isn't such a good idea," Sharon finally said. Cassie's lack of enthusiasm hurt, and suddenly she wondered if they were doing the right thing. "Maybe this is wrong. We don't have to go through with it. We can—"

"Sharon, if she's reacting like this with you, can you imagine what she would do with a stranger?" Grant leaned toward her, dark-blue eyes intense, words soft. "If you want out say so now, I'll understand. But I'm going to find a mother for Cassie."

His gaze seemed a physical touch that somehow drew an unwanted shimmer of awareness from her. An awareness of herself as a woman that surprised her. An awareness of Grant, very much a man, that disturbed her.

She pushed the unwelcome thoughts away with a frown—nerves, nothing more—and took a deep, calming breath. "I don't want out. I just...well, I expected her to be happy about it."

"She's not the only one who isn't happy," he said quietly.

Sharon's heart gave a painful lurch. "What—"

"I'm not talking about myself," he said with a half

smile that was nothing more than the lifting of one side of his mouth. "I called Hugh this morning. He was anything but delighted."

"Oh," she said softly. That hurt. "I liked Hugh and Dorothy when I met them, and it certainly would be easier if they accepted it...us."

"I don't think that's going to happen without a fight."

Her heart gave a hard jerk at his words. She suddenly realized how much she did want this marriage, how much she wanted to be Cassie's mother. "But we are still going through with the marriage?" she asked quietly.

"Absolutely." Grant ran a hand across his lean jaw. "We're doing this for Cassie, not to please Hugh and Dorothy." He shrugged. "They either get used to the idea, or they don't. It's not our problem." He paused. "As for Cassie...well, she's had a lot to deal with lately. She's probably just surprised. I'm sure she'll be happy, with a little time."

We could all use some time to get used to the idea. Sharon swallowed the words and tried to relax. "We don't have too much time," she reminded him. They were getting married by the weekend.

"It will work out," Grant said quietly. "We'll make it work."

During the week, Sharon was at the bank during the day, then at home packing in the evenings. A family who had lost all their possessions when their trailer burned two months earlier were recipients of most of her furniture, kitchen utensils and housewares. They came over Tuesday and Wednesday nights to help pack and move what they were taking.

Sharon couldn't avoid feeling some sadness, a sense of loss and dislocation, as the rooms in her little house slowly emptied, as she helped carry the worn but comfortable furniture into its new home and handed over the stoneware she'd had for years. Nothing fancy, all serviceable, and hers.

Then she pushed the sadness away. She didn't need any of these things. Grant's house lacked for nothing, and she was gaining a daughter. But she kept two small, oak bookshelves that she'd been meaning to refinish. Boxes of wellworn paperbacks. Her collection of clowns. The colorful throw pillows and afghans her grandmother had made and several nice prints she'd bought—though they were all different in hue from the pale, muted tones of Grant's house, she couldn't bear to part with them.

Thursday night, Grant came over and helped her move to his house. She spent the night in his guest bedroom, now her room. A restless, sleepless night that she thought would never end. She finally fell into an exhausted slumber by four o'clock in the morning. And overslept.

She jerked awake, disoriented and filled with the sense that something was wrong. She glanced at the clock and leaped out of bed. She had one hour to get Cassie ready and to day care, herself ready and to the courthouse. Grant would be no help, because he was in an early-morning meeting.

Disappointment stabbed her that Grant thought the meeting more important than their wedding. *Don't be silly,* she argued, digging out her shampoo. He would be there for the important part. And it wasn't as if this was a *real* marriage.

But it was to her, she realized with surprise. Not *real* real, but important. Very important. It would have been nice if Grant had canceled the meeting and driven with her to the courthouse.

For Grant to cancel a meeting, someone would have to be on his or her deathbed. And she did not have time to stand around and lament what could have been. The last thing she wanted was to be late.

She ran down the hall, nearly tripping over Brittany, who chased her, diving at her ankles, tail wagging furiously. "Cassie, get up." She knocked on the little girl's door, peeked inside. Cassie sat cross-legged in the middle of the bed, still in her pajamas, hair mussed. Brittany landed in her lap, and Cassie screeched with laughter.

"Could you please let Brittany out to potty and then get dressed? We have got to get you to day care." Cassie bounced off the bed with a grin, Brittany following. "And hurry," Sharon added. "We're late."

She was never late. Absolutely, positively, never.

Grant was pacing in the lobby of the courthouse when she rushed through the door with a minute to spare, helped by a gust of icy wind. "What a morning," she said, pushing windblown hair out of her eyes. He stopped and turned to face her, hands in his pockets, eyes dark. She froze at the intensity of his gaze.

"I thought you had changed your mind," he said quietly. A muscle tightened in his jaw.

Her heart squeezed at the uncertainty beneath Grant's quiet words. "I wouldn't do that to you, Grant. You should know that." She stepped closer, until the scent of his aftershave filled her nostrils. "You haven't changed your mind," she said, her words half question, half statement.

He hesitated. Her heart took an extra beat, then he slowly shook his head. He obviously wanted to, and that hurt. It shouldn't have, because she knew he was only doing this for Cassie, but it did anyway. A tiny stab directly to her heart. Another to her pride.

His gaze remained steady, eyes slightly narrowed, shoulders stiff. Dark suit, somber tie, unsmiling. A cold stranger who could not have looked more uncomfortable.

"We're getting married, not being sent to prison," she

said with a forced smile. *We should be happy,* she wanted to add. Instead, she swallowed the words as Grant slowly nodded, the muscle in his jaw tense. It might have been funny, except...well, somehow the humor just wasn't there. She suppressed a sigh of disappointment. And just a hint of anger.

"Give me a minute to comb my hair." She started to brush by him.

"Sharon..."

His low voice reached out and stopped her midstep. She slowly turned. Their gazes met and locked.

"I am sorry. I don't mean to act like an ass. It's just...well... This has got me tied in knots," he said in a husky voice.

Her heart ached for him. She reached to cup his jaw with her hand. A touch meant to reassure. She held his gaze. She couldn't be angry with him, even if she wanted to. She'd never been able to stay angry with Grant.

"We're both nervous, Grant. But you might want to keep in mind that we're in this together, by choice. We're friends, so let's try and be a little happy about it."

A vein throbbed in his brow. A thin line of blue against skin that used to sport a healthy tan but now didn't see the sun often enough because all Grant lived was work, day in, day out, month after month.

He needs her, she suddenly realized, and he doesn't even know it. Not only for Cassie, but for himself. Her heart took an extra beat at the thought. And then she straightened her shoulders.

"Forget the hair," she said softly. "It won't look much different even if I do comb it, and I believe we have an appointment we don't want to be late for, Mr. Parker."

She pointed an elbow at Grant. He gave her a crooked smile, then slipped his arm through hers, and they turned as one toward their new destiny.

* * *

The ceremony was simple, no nonsense, to be performed in the office of the marriage commissioner, a slender woman who looked far too young to have the authority to legally tie a man and woman to each other. The ceremony would be such a contrast to his first wedding—an extravagant, formal affair—that Grant didn't expect to think of Catherine. To mentally compare the huge diamond Catherine had insisted upon with the simple gold wedding band waiting in his pocket for Sharon.

Though he tried to push the memories away, they slipped through him. The buoyant hopes and dreams that had slowly dampened and died over the years, ending in pain and despair, disillusionment. And along with those hopes and dreams went his capacity to love, killed by the crushing reality of his failure at marriage, by his inability to keep Catherine happy.

What the hell was he doing getting married again? Cold washed through him, and suddenly he couldn't move. Could not speak or even look at Sharon. Wanted nothing more than to turn and run from the room, fleeing the murmur of words.

And then there was silence.

"Grant?"

Sharon's soft voice slid through the cold to pull his gaze to hers. Thickly lashed eyes shining with compassion and trust. This was Sharon, his friend, the sister he'd never had. He took a deep breath and then another. She would not let him down. And they did not love each other except as long-lasting friends, so he couldn't fail her. The fear slowly subsided as he dug in his pocket for the ring.

He slipped the band on Sharon's finger. She had a small, square hand, lightly freckled. He refused to compare it with Catherine's. More words. Then Sharon reached for Grant's hand to return the favor with a plain gold band that matched hers.

Her warm smile reached out as if it were a physical touch. A touch that drew an immediate awareness of her flushed cheeks. They curved against warm skin to end at soft, kissable lips, inviting a man to lightly trace them from the cheekbone down. Any thought of Catherine fled. Gone was his safe and familiar friend, replaced in a heartbeat by a stranger. A very attractive, desirable woman.

He jerked his gaze away to the marriage commissioner, heart pounding. And then they were pronounced man and wife. The words "You may kiss the bride" echoed in the sudden silence. Grant slowly turned, breath painfully caught. Sharon tilted her head, then grinned and winked. In that instant, the stranger fled and the stranglehold on his breathing released.

This was Sharon. His best friend.

This was Grant, her best friend, offering nothing more than a friendly kiss to seal a bargain, Sharon told herself as he slowly lowered his head. Her eyes fluttered shut; her breath caught as his lips settled against hers. The soft, gentle kiss ended far too quickly and left her pulse racing.

She opened her eyes to meet his gaze. A puzzled gaze that clung to her lips like a touch and had her heart hammering wildly. A heartbeat of shimmering awareness seemed to hang between them. Her breath caught. And then Grant cleared his throat and stepped back. The moment died so quickly she wondered if she had imagined it.

They thanked the marriage commissioner, gathered their paperwork, then turned as one and left, stopping in the hall. Grant cleared his throat again. "Well, I guess that's it." His smile was a bit strained, the silence between them stiff, uncomfortable, as if the ceremony had suddenly changed them. Dropped a wall of self-consciousness between them.

She refused to let that happen.

"Who'd have thought..." Sharon smiled when he met her gaze. "Twenty-five dollars and three days is all you need to get a wife or a husband. And they say there are no bargains."

One corner of his mouth curved up in a half smile. She reached to touch him lightly on the arm as she'd done hundreds of times throughout their childhood, yet this time it was different. This was her husband.

No, she immediately corrected herself. Well, yes and no. It did not matter that they were husband and wife. This was her dearest friend and their marriage was not going to affect that friendship.

She wrapped her arm with his and leaned against him slightly. "Remember in third grade when we got married in the backyard? And we used rubber bands for rings?"

"Damned near lost the circulation in my finger because you wanted me to wear it forever, and I didn't want to let you down." He smiled. "Kids." He shook his head, still grinning. "Some of the things we did."

A game for him. The beginning of unrequited love for her, she couldn't help thinking.

Unrequited love. She snorted inwardly at the thought and told herself to quit being so melodramatic. That was all part of the past, and she had long gotten over her feelings for Grant. She returned his smile. "Shall we go get a late breakfast to celebrate?"

His smile died. "I can't, Sharon. I'm sorry, but I'm supposed to meet some folks in a couple of minutes."

But this is our wedding morning. Can't you forget work for just a while? She swallowed the words.

"Okay. I'll see you tonight then," she said, stepping back to release him.

He hesitated, then nodded, turned and strode down the hall and out of sight.

* * *

The house resisted Sharon with a deep, heavy silence. If not for Brittany's ecstatic welcome, she would have been tempted to turn and leave. Silly, but true. She stepped inside tentatively, as if she were a thief, and stood for one long minute in the kitchen. Grant's kitchen. The furnace in the garage came to life with a rumble, startling her. It sounded so very different from her own—

No. She stopped the thought. She wasn't going to compare this place with the little house that now waited for the next renter. She took a deep breath, then headed for her room to slip out of her dress, into jeans faded with age and a baggy sweatshirt that had long ago lost its shape. She was determined to think only positive thoughts.

Yet the house seemed to defy her resolve with a heavy, unwelcoming silence, broken only by the rustle of newspaper as she unpacked and the occasional snort or whimper from Brittany as she lay dreaming on the foot of the bed.

Catherine's house, not yours, the silence seemed to whisper. Grant had designed and built and furnished this for Catherine. *She* hadn't felt herself an interloper the way Sharon did as she entered a room, or walked the hall, or touched the brightly polished faucets in the bathroom that separated her room from Cassie's.

You're being silly, Sharon told herself, then reached for another box. It will just take some time to get used to living here. It's a large, well-designed house filled with new furniture, carpet that invited bare feet and most everything a person could need or hope for. In fact, it looked like a house from a magazine, picture perfect.

So why did it feel so cold and empty? Brittany snorted again. Sharon smiled. Snort, indeed. The pup was unwittingly right. There was nothing wrong with the house that a little love and laughter couldn't cure. And that would take time.

She pulled her own soft flannel sheets out of a box and

made the bed, topping it with a quilt, once vibrant with color, now faded from many washings. She frowned at the elaborate bedspread now lying at her feet, then carefully folded it and took it down the hall to the linen closet. Not that there was anything wrong with the spread. It just wasn't her. She wanted something homey and warm. Comfortable. And something that was hers.

She pushed her old cedar chest onto a piece of cardboard, then dragged it in from the garage and parked it in a corner. It needed refinishing, looked a shabby third cousin to the oak dresser sitting nearby. She dismissed the thought, then unpacked the brightly colored afghans, stacked them on top of the cedar chest. She put the box of throw pillows by the side, not certain Grant would want them strewn around the house, yet reluctant to part with them.

Soon the closet was full of her clothes, as was the dresser. She toyed with the idea of dragging in the bookshelves, but there simply wasn't room, so the boxes of books remained against the wall for now and her collection of clowns stayed in their cardboard prison.

She hung two prints—strong, vibrant Alaskan landscapes—on one wall. The others she leaned in the bottom of the closet. Then she stepped back to survey the room. It had come alive with splashes of rich color here and there, and had a more comfortable air with the faded quilt and the battered cedar chest.

Enough damage done for one day, she thought, glancing at her watch. She would go get Cassie early.

They had discussed having Cassie at the brief ceremony, then decided it would be easier for all if she went to day care as she normally did. That way, Sharon would have time to unpack and settle in without interruption. Cassie had seemed perfectly happy with the decision, Sharon remembered with a sinking heart.

She would feel a whole lot better about things if Cassie were more excited. Even a little excited would do at this point. If only the child would tell them what was bothering her, because something clearly was. And Sharon felt as though her emotions were on a yo-yo, as Cassie alternated between being her old loving self and maintaining a cool distance, watching Sharon with careful, somber eyes.

Maybe having the afternoon free to spend time with her would do the trick. Excitement and hope spiraled through Sharon as she hurried to the garage, Brittany trotting at her heels.

The wind had died, the clouds now blown away. The rugged mountains that ringed Valdez were filled with glaring snow, blinding to look at without sunglasses. They sliced a space for themselves in the brilliant blue sky.

The air was sharp and biting, although the ravens perched on the side of a large, green Dumpster didn't seem to notice. They cocked their heads, fixing a glittering, beady-eyed stare on Sharon as she drove by.

She took a deep breath as she pulled to a stop in front of the day care a couple of seconds later. She was, she realized, officially a mother, picking up her own child. Cassie's mother.

Emotion swept through her, emotions so intense she could not move for one long minute. Would Cassie ever think of her as her mother, call her "mother"? Her throat constricted at the thought. Then Brittany woofed, reached over and nosed her hand, as if to say, go on in there and get Cassie. What are you waiting for?

Sharon smiled and ruffled the fur on the pup's head. What, indeed? She nearly sprang from the car, her step light and quick as she hurried into the building.

Cassie was more subdued than usual. She didn't even respond with her usual happy giggles when Brittany insisted on sitting next to her in the bucket seat, nearly flattening the little girl against the door.

"Is everything okay?" Sharon asked as she inched the car onto the icy street.

Cassie turned a far too solemn gaze toward her. "Yeah." Then she turned back to look out the window.

"No problems at day care?" Sharon persisted, trying to resist a sinking heart. Visions of black eyes flashed to mind. Of permanent residence in the time-out room. But Cassie shook her head without turning.

Sharon tried again. "Are you feeling sick?" Another silent shake of the head offered little encouragement.

Sharon paused. "I thought that we could make chocolate chip cookies when we got home. And then make spaghetti and meatballs for dinner." Cassie's favorites.

Cassie shrugged, her gaze still riveted out the window, and Sharon's heart did sink. A knot of disappointment, of worry, tightened in her stomach, bringing with it an encompassing ache.

"Cassie, are you mad that I married your dad?" she asked softly.

The little girl didn't answer for one long minute. Long enough for Sharon's heart to drop somewhere close to her toes.

"No, I'm not mad," Cassie finally said.

She spoke so quietly that Sharon almost didn't hear her. Somehow the words, the tone of voice, were not reassuring.

"Then what is wrong?" she asked gently.

Cassie ignored the question, nose still pressed to the window. The only reason Sharon didn't pull the car over right then and there and insist that the girl talk was that she knew Cassie possessed the same bullheaded streak Grant had. Nothing short of threat of death, and maybe not even that, would make the little girl talk until she was ready.

The rest of the drive home was filled with a damning silence.

When they pulled into the garage, Cassie slid from the car and went to her room, taking Brittany and the last bit of Sharon's hope with her. She stayed there the rest of the afternoon, coming out once for some orange juice.

Sharon started the cookies, thinking that maybe the smell would entice the little girl, and ended up finishing the batch by herself. Surrounded by the unwelcoming silence of a kitchen that was not her own. Stepmother to a daughter who apparently did not want her.

Rather than being able to bury himself in work, Grant had to endure endless backslapping, congratulations and teasing about what he was doing at work when he should be off on a honeymoon.

He couldn't set them straight, so he forced a smile and reminded them that he was too busy to honeymoon now. Maybe he would when the project was finished. Cassie needed to be with them as a family far more than they needed a honeymoon. The excuses sounded as flimsy and feeble as they were—or would have been, had his marriage been real.

He finally filled his briefcase with work and fled, relieved to escape his staff and co-workers. The relief was short-lived as the knot in his stomach grew larger, tighter, with each passing mile that pulled him closer to town. Through town and closer to home.

Home and a new wife.

It's only Sharon, he reminded himself. It wasn't as if she was a real wife. The gold wedding band flashed in the dim light of the cab as it rested against the steering wheel, and seemed to grip his finger in a tight, cold hold. It felt like a real wedding band.

The pickup turned almost of its own volition and he started up the hill to the house. The knot in his stomach twisted tighter.

Light spilled from the house windows in welcome, painting the driveway and snow with mellow light and shadow and giving the building life. Sharon's compact station wagon squatted in the garage stall he normally used. Warmth, light, the sound of soft music and the smell of dinner cooking greeted him as he swung open the door.

The atmosphere was so different from the cool silence he had become used to that he stopped briefly, disconcerted in spite of himself. Then he stepped inside, closing the door behind. He toed off his shoes, carefully arranging them beneath the bench. Slowly hung his jacket. Put his briefcase on the bench.

When he realized he was stalling, strangely reluctant to walk farther into the house, he frowned and went into the kitchen. And found Sharon setting the table, alone.

His heart tightened. "Sharon?" She looked at him with eyes so bruised and sad that fear clutched him. "What's wrong?" He took a step closer.

Sharon dropped her gaze, then shook her head. "Nothing," she said quietly. "I'm just a little tired, that's all." She looked up again. "Cassie doesn't seem to want to have anything to do with me."

Her need for comfort pulled at him.

He froze. Something close to panic fluttered in his stomach; every muscle in his body tightened. He should go to her. He couldn't. It seemed as if his feet were suddenly cemented to the floor. His tongue was thick and unwieldy, his mouth full of tundra cotton.

This is Sharon, he told himself. Your friend. You've

offered her comfort a million times over the years, for everything from scraped knees to broken hearts.

He forced himself to slowly walk forward, to place a large hand on her shoulder. She turned into him, and his arms settled around her as naturally as if they belonged there.

She was warm and soft and—

He pushed the thought away, unfinished, resisted an urge to pull back, his heart thudding in his chest. He swallowed hard, and forced himself to stay. Offering all that he could at the moment by tightening his fingers, while an encompassing ache crept through him. An ache of fear? Regret? Of emotion long dead? He had no answers, no time to think any out.

Sharon finally stepped back, straightening her shoulders. "Enough of that." She smiled a wan smile. "Could you have Cassie wash up? Dinner will be ready in ten minutes."

And then she turned her attention back to the stove, releasing him.

Leaving him with a sense of emptiness he did not understand. And was not sure he wanted to.

Chapter Four

Dinner was a quiet affair, strained silence the main course. Nothing like what Sharon had imagined. No warmth, no laughter. Instead, it was almost as if they were strangers, stiff and awkward, when they should have been relaxed and filling the kitchen with happy chatter.

Exhaustion swept her—the culmination of an emotion-laden week and a rotten afternoon. She didn't think she had the energy to deal with anything else, but knew she had to see the evening through. A throb in her brow threatened to turn into a full-blown headache.

Cassie played with her food more than she ate, and avoided looking at Sharon. Grant ate, but shot shuttered glances at both of them, eyes shadowed with darkness that seemed to deepen in direct proportion to the silence in the kitchen. Sharon racked her brain, as she had all afternoon, for reasons Cassie would be angry with her, and found none.

The loving little girl who had turned to her so often in the past was gone, and Sharon did not know how to get her back. She had expected some awkward moments while she settled in, until Cassie adjusted to the idea of her being here, but nothing like this.

The silence continued, growing more unbearable by the minute, broken only by the clang of cutlery against plates. Cassie cut a meatball into pieces, then began to slowly and methodically mash it. Nerves stretched taut, Sharon couldn't stand any more. "If you're done, I'll take that." She whisked Cassie's plate out from under her nose.

Cassie stared at her, eyes wide, fork suspended in mid-air, mouth open with surprise. Grant arched a brow, looked at Cassie and then back at Sharon. Her breath caught. He had to be as disappointed as she was, if not more. The thought that she was letting him down, on top of all else, was almost her undoing.

"Dinner was excellent," he said quietly. "We'll help with the dishes."

"No." Sharon almost cried the words. "I'd rather do them alone." She wanted nothing more than to be alone. Alone in her own little house would have been preferable, but since it wasn't possible, she wanted both Grant and Cassie out of the room. If she had to endure silence, at least let it be her own. Grant arched a brow, opened his mouth as if to argue. "Please," she added.

"Okay," he finally agreed. "We'll be in the family room."

She felt guilt at the relief that flooded her when they left, Cassie racing to release Brittany from the prison of Sharon's bedroom. But she desperately needed some time alone to try to repair frayed nerves. To think.

So what if Cassie had suddenly decided Sharon was her mortal enemy? There had to be a reason for it that she was missing. And being a mature, responsible adult, she could handle it.

She put food away, loaded the dishwasher and cleaned

and wiped down the counters, until she realized she had done them twice and was just wasting time. She piled a plate high with freshly baked chocolate chip cookies, squared her shoulders and headed toward the family room. She would not retire to her room and bawl her eyes out the way she wanted. Tears never solved anything. She would face the evening straight on, and maybe, just maybe, Cassie would warm up enough so she could find out what was bothering the girl.

A fire snapped and crackled on the grate, offering warmth and comfort with its cheery lick of flame. Brittany sprawled in front of it, asleep. Grant lay on the couch, Cassie sitting squarely on his flat stomach, fiddling with the buttons on his shirt. Sharon stepped into the room, caught Grant's eye just as Cassie spoke.

"Daddy, do I have to call Sharon 'Mama'?" she asked in a low voice.

Pain shot through Sharon. She nearly dropped the cookies. Grant's eyes widened, jerked to the little girl, then back to Sharon. Cassie stiffened, apparently sensing Sharon's presence.

Sharp disappointment resonated through Sharon. She carefully set the cookies on the coffee table, then settled on the love seat, wrapping trembling fingers together in her lap.

"No. You can continue calling her 'Sharon' if that's what you want," Grant finally answered, turning his attention back to Cassie.

Sharon waited, muscles aching with tension. She was uncertain what to say, if anything. Cassie slowly turned to face her, brows drawn together, face stiff and withdrawn, almost unrecognizable. Sharon wanted to cry out, to pull the girl to her and insist that she tell them what was wrong. Tell them what had robbed her of her smile and Sharon of her love. Instead, she pushed the almost overwhelming disappointment away with a hard swallow.

"Your daddy is right, Cass. You don't have to call me anything that you don't want," she finally said quietly.

Cassie dropped her gaze. The rigid set of her features did not soften. Silence filled the room, broken by a sudden pop of a log on the fire. And then Grant spoke.

"But since Sharon is married to me now, she is your stepmother. You—"

Cassie twisted from Grant's lap with a violent jerk, landing on her feet and stepping back, hands on her hips, face contorted with emotion. "She is *not* my mother," she hollered. "*My* mother is dead."

Grant's mouth dropped open and he sat up. Sharon felt blood drain from her face in a cold rush. Pain exploded inside her chest. She bit her lip to keep from crying out. Brittany leaped to her feet, tail tucked. Then Cassie whirled and ran from the room. Brittany hesitated, then raced after her. The slam of a door reverberated through the house a few seconds later.

Grant stared at Sharon. "Do you have any idea what that was all about?" He enunciated each word, looking as shocked as she felt.

Sharon shook her head, not trusting her voice. Chills trembled through her. Hot tears threatened to fill her eyes, and a cold knot the size of a boulder filled her chest. "I suppose we should have expected something like this." She forced the words out.

"Not like this," he immediately disagreed. "Not this strong a reaction. She loves you, Sharon. We both know that, without a minute of doubt. Sure, she's going to have some adjusting to do— we all are." He paused. "But this is not anything I anticipated," he said slowly.

He swung to his feet. "I'll go talk to her and—"

"No," Sharon said quickly. She fought to speak in a

steady voice. "Let's give her a few minutes and then I'll go." She drew a deep breath. "After all, I'm the one she's having a problem with." Her voice wavered.

"This is not your fault."

She tried to smile, to believe him, but couldn't. At the moment, she wanted nothing more than to bury herself in his arms as she had many times when she was a little girl, and pretend that none of this was happening.

She couldn't. Neither one of them was a child anymore. So she remained silent, seated alone, wondering what she had truly gotten herself into. Had she been so blind that she had been unable to see past her love for Cassie, past her own selfish needs? Unable to recognize that marriage to Grant was not the answer for anyone?

A deep, encompassing cold swept through Grant. It felt as if a heavy fist settled in his chest, wrapping an iron-clad grip around his heart, his lungs. Sharon looked at the floor, as if she could not stand to look at him. As if he were somehow failing her, failing both of them.

Shades of the past that struck him a bitter blow.

This can't be happening, he thought. I married Sharon to make Cassie happy. Instead, Cassie seemed to want nothing to do with Sharon. And Sharon was miserable.

Life suddenly took on a nightmarish quality.

If you can't keep a wife happy, how can you be a good parent?

Hugh's words slashed through Grant as the sour taste of failure filled his mouth, its stench poisoning the air. Hugh was right, he thought in a moment of panic. Sweat dotted his brow as a shudder ran through him. He was failing once again. Not only himself and Cassie, but Sharon.

Sharon, by virtue of becoming his wife, had also become his responsibility. Intended or not. His bones chilled to the marrow.

"I'm sorry," she murmured. "I thought she loved me. I didn't...did not expect...this."

Each word stabbed at him, jerking him to his feet. He settled next to Sharon on the love seat, aching to make things better but not certain he could. "Sharon?" he said in a husky voice.

She stared at her hands. "Maybe I'm just not meant to be a mother," she whispered hoarsely.

"This has nothing to do with you, with your ability as a parent." His denial was as automatic as it was emphatic. He reached to clasp her hands, heart beating faster than normal.

She turned to him with a moan and curled against his chest. "How do you know?" she cried, voice muffled against his shoulder, tears soaking his shirt.

His arms folded around her, their bodies fitting together as if one. "I just do," he said through a tight throat. "You know that Cassie loves you. You've been a mother to her since...even before Catherine died." His hands traveled the length of her back in large circles, as they automatically did when he soothed Cassie. "You will be—*are* a good mother. Don't ever doubt that."

She burrowed closer. A myriad of sensations, of images, rushed through him. She was warm, soft, and clung to him as if he could somehow right a world suddenly turned topsy-turvy. He only wished he could. And knew from past experience that it was an impossible task.

"But maybe—"

"Maybe, nothing," he said firmly. He had to make her believe. "I don't know why Cassie is acting this way, but it has nothing to do with your ability to be a parent. Nothing."

Silence fell upon them as the clock slowly ticked away the minutes. Grant held Sharon, his hold on her tightening when he felt her shudder against him.

"Thank you," she whispered against his neck. She pulled back and met his gaze with red-rimmed eyes.

He tilted her chin with his finger. "You do believe me, don't you?"

She hesitated, then cautiously nodded. "I'll go talk to Cassie now."

She walked slowly from the room. Leaving him there, alone, arms empty. He clenched his hands as if to erase the feel of her beneath them. As if to somehow force the memory of how she felt in his arms away, also. Then he expelled a pent-up breath.

He couldn't help but wonder if this marriage of convenience wasn't going to complicate his life more than solve problems.

Cassie was pretending to sleep, eyes tightly shut, lips clamped in a thin line. Brittany wiggled from beneath her bony elbow and danced toward Sharon as she set the milk and cookies on the nightstand, then settled on the edge of the bed.

She scratched the pup's silken ears, giving Cassie time to decide to stop the charade. "You know," she said, "it really is okay to call me 'Sharon.'" Silence. "I thought we were friends, best friends." Still silence. "Friends work things out, Cassie. And in order to do that, they have to talk to each other when things are bothering them."

Sharon glanced at the little girl. Both eyes were still squeezed shut. She suppressed a sigh. "Just because I'm your stepmother now doesn't mean I'm trying to replace Catherine, Cass. In fact, I would never want you to forget your mother. Ever."

A tear leaked from Cassie's eye. Sharon's heart filled with compassion. "Cassie?" she said softly, resting a hand gently on a slightly trembling shoulder.

Silence, but another tear slid out.

Then Cassie opened her eyes. She swallowed hard. "Are you mad at me, Sharon?"

Her voice quavered and broke, nearly breaking Sharon's heart in the process. "No, little goose, I am not mad at you," Sharon answered. "I love you too much to be mad, and you didn't do anything wrong." She paused, then held out an arm. "Need a hug as much as I do?"

The little girl moaned, then twisted and climbed into Sharon's arms. She burrowed against Sharon's neck and sobbed, great shuddering sobs that ripped chunks out of Sharon's heart.

"Shhh," Sharon soothed. "It's okay. Everything is going to be all right," she murmured over and over again.

Cassie's tears soaked Sharon's shirt. She didn't care, only hugged the trembling girl closer, tighter, as if somehow the action would make the world right once more. Finally, exhaustion won out and Cassie's sobs grew softer, dispersed with a hiccup or two, and then she relaxed against Sharon and slept.

Sharon held her for a few minutes longer, then settled her back in bed, pulled the covers up and pressed a kiss to her heated brow. Brittany immediately planted her head next to Cassie's on the pillow and begged with her eyes to stay.

"I can tell whose dog you're going to be, and I don't blame you one bit," she whispered, then gathered the milk and cookies. She paused for one last look before closing the door on the sleeping child and puppy, filled with a sudden hope that tomorrow would be better.

The scream jerked Grant from a solid sleep. He was on his feet and down the hall in seconds, wearing only pajama bottoms. Another scream sliced the air and he ran harder.

He rounded the corner of Cassie's room. Sharon sat on the edge of the bed, Cassie cuddled in her arms as she rocked her and soothed her. Sharon glanced up at Grant, eyes wide and dark in a pale face.

Cassie gasped on a sob and let out another bloodcurdling scream. Sharon jumped. Grant swore. Brittany cowered at the foot of the bed. Grant strode forward without thought, pulled Cassie from Sharon into a hug, keeping the child's chin nestled on his shoulder.

"She's not awake," he said more curtly than he'd intended, and was rewarded with another shriek that nearly split his eardrum. He swore and jerked back. "Cassie, it's okay. Wake up." He gave her a small shake. "Wake up, Cass. It's Daddy."

She opened her mouth as if to scream again, then blinked once, twice, shook her head like a startled bird, then closed her mouth, finally awake. He dropped into the large rocker in the corner and tucked her beneath his chin. "Bad dream?" he soothed, rocking back and forth in rhythm with the shudders of her small body.

"Yeah," she finally responded, then nestled closer.

They rocked in silence until Sharon spoke. "Is she okay?" she asked quietly. She still sat on the bed, Brittany at her side. Pale, shaken, eyes dark with emotion.

"Just a bad dream. She'll be fine," Grant said. "You can go on to bed now."

Her brows drew together in a frown. She opened her mouth as if to say something, hesitated, then dropped her gaze and nodded. Slowly, as if an old woman, she stood. She paused at the door and glanced back, eyes filled with reproach, then walked from the room without a word, Brittany at her heels.

Her reproach slapped at Grant as if it were a physical blow. He silently muttered an oath at the wave of immediate guilt he felt. He was just so used to doing things on his own. But that was no excuse. Sharon was now a part of his life, his family. His responsibility.

The memory of her in his arms earlier that evening reared up. The beat of her heart, the warmth, her silken hair pressed against his cheek, and her scent—

He took a deep breath, shoved the memory away and any meaning it might have. Cassie shifted, muttered and burrowed against him. He pushed Sharon out of his mind and focused entirely on his daughter.

Because he knew how to do that. And because it was safe.

When Cassie finally slept, he tucked her in, then went in search of Sharon. He didn't know if he felt more guilty because she was in her room, door closed, or because he could not help the small surge of relief that the apology could wait until morning.

A dark, clear sky greeted Sharon when she awoke. Faint stars winked through the parted curtains. It would be a cold, bright day when the sun finally made an appearance.

Instead of rising and dressing with her normal eagerness, Sharon lay still, lethargic, filled with an unsettled heaviness from a restless night. And the memory of yesterday. The memory of Cassie's nightmare, of Grant jerking her from Sharon's arms.

Cassie had never had a nightmare while at her house, so how could she know the little girl was not awake? The memory of his terse words was as painful as when they were spoken. He hadn't meant to hurt her—of that she was certain. But the unconscious act had clearly drawn the line: he and Cassie on one side, she on the other. And this was something she had never once considered.

Lying in bed, moping, was accomplishing nothing. And maybe today would be better, she told herself, then rolled from bed with a sigh. It could hardly get worse.

She made a trip outside for Brittany and then took a

shower. Dressed in an oversized flannel shirt and leggings, Sharon was ready to face the world.

The aroma of fresh-brewed coffee greeted her in the kitchen. Grant leaned against the counter next to the coffeepot, sipping a steaming mug. Whiskers shadowed his jaw; his thick hair looked tousled, as if only finger-combed. He was oddly appealing. Her heart skipped a beat.

Faded jeans molded his hips and long, well-muscled legs. A T-shirt of gun-metal gray stretched across his shoulders and chest, accentuating his dark, good looks.

The memory of being held in his arms returned full strength. The feeling of being safe, of being comforted for just a few minutes. And the simple pleasure of being held by a man once again. This was a direction her thoughts did not need to take, she told herself with a frown. Grant was her friend, and she did not think of friends in that manner.

His eyes captured her and her heart skipped another beat. He slowly set the coffee mug aside.

"I owe you an apology for last night," he said in a low voice. "I didn't mean to push you away like that." He paused, then added, "It won't happen again."

At those few words, a slow smile flowered from within. Suddenly, the day looked brighter, full of hope. "Apology accepted," she said softly, then walked over to stand next to him and pour herself some coffee.

The phone rang. He turned to answer it, the seams of his T-shirt straining against well-defined muscle. She could almost feel the heat from his body. His musky scent filled her nostrils.

Desire swept her, unexpected, unwanted, every inch of her body suddenly on fire with pure and simple physical awareness. Every cell attuned to the fact that Grant was a man, a very attractive man in his prime. And that she was a woman.

She froze, resisting the urge to turn and flee the room. As if by so doing, she could deny the desire, the weakness in her limbs, the reality that she wanted Grant, in a way and strength she was totally unprepared for. And absolutely did not want.

Running never accomplished anything, she told herself. Besides, where would she run? No, she had to stay and face this unexpected turn of events and conquer it.

A slow spiral of steam rose from the dark liquid in the mug she clasped between her hands as if it were a lifeline. The rumble of Grant's voice sent a shiver down her spine. She took several deep breaths, finally raised her mug with hands that still trembled slightly and took a very long swallow of coffee. Desperately needing strength and hoping the caffeine would provide it.

What in the world was wrong with her? Although she had long recognized that Grant was an attractive man, he was an attractive man who hadn't looked twice at her over the years, she reminded herself. Not only did she not want this frighteningly intense surge of awareness of him, it could not happen again.

If he knew...

He wouldn't, she told herself. And it would not happen again, she silently added, and hoped that she was right. She drew a determined breath, then another. Her reaction...overreaction had to be because she was tired.

She took another deep breath, then forced herself to turn, to run her gaze the length of his body. Nothing happened. No heart stopping. No pulse racing. Nothing more than her normal, uneventful reaction at seeing Grant. Relief flooded her, along with a renewed sense of hope.

She turned toward the table. And stopped. Cassie stood in the kitchen door, staring at Sharon. Sharon's heart tripped for just a second, then she smiled. "Good morning, little goose," she said softly.

For a minute, a very short minute, Cassie smiled. Her old smile, eyes filled with love and welcome. Then her eyes shuttered, her smile died. "Good morning," she said quietly, then walked over to the table.

And Sharon knew with a sinking heart that it was not a good morning at all.

Grant's eyes seemed to have a mind of their own. They watched every move Sharon made as she went from cupboard to cupboard, to the fridge and back to the counter, in the process of making waffles. He looked away. Seconds later his eyes wandered back to her, like a magnet to metal.

The aroma of baking waffles soon filled the room, but Grant barely noticed. Instead, he strove to listen to his construction supervisor, while he watched Sharon. Her rust-and-gold-toned oversized flannel shirt should have hidden every curve but only seemed to accentuate them. Her slender legs were hugged by a pair of chocolate brown leggings.

His heart took an unexpected extra beat. He frowned, did not have time to analyze his reaction as she brushed by him. The clean scent of soap, shampoo and perfume filled his nostrils. Her shirt stretched across her chest as she reached on tiptoe to get plates, and crept up her thighs to almost reveal—

He jerked his gaze away, disturbingly aware of her as a woman. He turned and took a quick step to distance himself, and almost strangled himself with the phone cord.

His back to Sharon, he forced himself to listen to the conversation, and fought to ignore her presence. Finally, he concluded the call, wondering if he'd remember any of it and how much of it he'd missed.

He faced her. "Can I help?" His voice was low and husky.

Sharon shot him a startled look. He flushed, cleared his

throat. She shook her head. "I'm almost through. Have a seat."

Cassie sat at the table, waffle on her plate drowning in a lake of syrup.

"Like some waffle with that syrup?" Grant pulled out a chair and winked at her.

"Oh, Daddy!" Cassie grinned at him.

Then Sharon walked over and set a plate of waffles in the middle of the table. Cassie's grin died. She looked down at her plate. Sharon took a seat and tried to smile at both of them. But her gaze lingered on Cassie, her smile turning to a grimace of bewildered sadness.

Grant's heart sank. Weariness swept him. He did not know what to do to mend things between Cassie and Sharon. He wasn't even sure how to get his daughter to talk about it. He carefully buttered a waffle. They ate in silence for a minute. "That was some bad dream you had last night, Cass," he finally said.

She jerked her gaze to his. For just a minute, fear flashed in her eyes. Grant frowned. "Do you remember what it was about?"

She hesitated, then slowly shook her head, dropping her gaze back to her plate. *She knows,* doubt whispered in his mind. "Are you sure you don't remember?"

Cassie hesitated again, then nodded without looking at him. And Grant could tell she was lying. A hard, cold fist clenched in his stomach. To the best of his knowledge, Cassie had never felt the need to lie to him before.

He watched his daughter toy with a piece of waffle for one long minute, then he turned his gaze to Sharon. She watched Cassie with a look as troubled as he felt.

The phone rang, a shrill that demanded to be answered.

"That's probably work." Grant pushed back from the table. The problems of a multimillion-dollar project seemed minor in comparison with what faced him at the table.

"Grant, Hugh here."

He fought the urge to hang up at the familiar voice. At the rush of tension it brought.

"Grant? Grant? Are you there?"

"I'm here," Grant finally said, each word carefully spoken.

"I thought maybe you had hung up on me." Hugh paused. Grant remained silent. "Well…" Hugh cleared his throat and then continued. "Well, I just thought I would call and see how things are."

"Things are fine."

"Ah, I see," Hugh said after a short silence. "And…ah, Sharon? How is she?"

Grant fought an immediate welling of anger that Hugh would even ask, as if he cared. "Sharon is fine, also," he said in a voice chilled by at least two degrees.

Hugh sighed. "You can't blame us for worrying, Grant. I mean, it's only natural." His tone cooled. "This marriage was awful hasty and we're not convinced that it's in Cassie's best interest. You—"

"We'd better end this conversation now," Grant said in a cold, hard growl. He struggled to control the anger that raged through him.

Silence.

"Would you like to talk to Cassie?" Grant could barely force the words out. Cassie shot him a questioning look when he called her to the phone. Sharon frowned when he joined her at the table.

"Do you think you needed to be that tough on him?" she half whispered.

"Yes," he said abruptly. Sharon arched a brow as if she were going to question him, but didn't. He almost continued, then stopped. He didn't want Sharon worrying, somehow blaming herself for Hugh's ugly reaction and continuing resistance to the marriage. He would tell her later, when they got Cassie straightened out. Besides, there wasn't a whole lot Hugh could do other than bluster and disapprove, and finally accept the situation.

With his appetite gone, the soggy waffle on the plate looked anything but inviting. He pushed it back.

"Have a fresh—"

"No." The single word stopped Sharon, fork poised above the stack of waffles. Eyes wide, worried. A slight flush coloring her cheeks. He fought a sudden urge to reach out, to trail a finger along her jaw, to wipe the flush from her soft skin.

Instead, he pushed back from the table.

"I've got some paperwork I need to do."

Sharon's gaze followed him from the room. He could feel it as clearly as if it were a physical touch.

Sharon found Grant in his den, head bent over a pile of paperwork, oblivious to the sunshine streaming through the window. She hesitated, then knocked. His head jerked up. Dark shadows smudged below his eyes. Shadows she had not noticed earlier.

"May I?" She sat in a chair opposite him, aching to know what to say, to do, to help him. Cassie clearly had not forgiven her whatever sin Sharon had committed. Grant had obviously been upset by talking with Hugh. He was a man inundated with problems. Problems she was supposed to help solve, not add to.

"I talked with Hugh," she said quietly. Grant didn't respond, so she continued. "He seemed a little concerned over Cassie's lack of enthusiasm about our marriage."

"He said that to you! The—"

"Only in a roundabout way," she quickly assured him. "We spoke briefly. Very briefly." Grant remained silent.

"He...well, he indicated he and Dorothy might come up for a visit. Soon." She paused. "I told him they were more than welcome. I hope you don't mind, but I thought that maybe it would set his mind at ease."

"I doubt it." Grant's eyes darkened. His mouth thinned and a muscle in his jaw tightened. "But it doesn't much matter, does it? We are married, and there isn't a damned thing they can do about it. They can't take Cassie so they will just have to get used to the idea. And I am not sure I want either of them in my house."

"Grant." Sharon protested. "They're Cassie's grandparents. And regardless how you might feel, she needs them."

"I know that," he said in a husky voice, then turned to look out the window, eyes glittering, shoulders rigid.

Sharon's stomach tightened in an ache. He looked so...alone. "I'm sorry, Grant," she apologized. "I did my best."

"This is not your fault," he answered.

One long minute stretched between them. Grant remained silent, eyes trained out the window, shutting the world out. And Sharon with it.

That hurt, and it shouldn't have. At least not as badly as it did. She took a deep breath, knowing that the task ahead was next to impossible, determined to try regardless. "It's an awfully nice day out."

He finally turned back to face her. "Yes, it is." He picked up his pen.

"Good day for sledding, don't you think?" she quickly added.

"That's an excellent idea. You two have fun." He dropped his attention back to the paperwork. She didn't move, did not say a word. He slowly raised his head, brow arched.

"I meant the three of us," she said quietly. "Well, four,

if you count Brittany.'' She tried a smile. His brow arched farther. She sighed. "Come on, Grant, you need to get out and do things with Cassie. If not for her, for yourself. You can't bury yourself in work forever.''

His brow arched higher. She ignored it. "And you're not blind. Do you honestly think that Cassie is going to want to go with me?''

He slowly put his pen down. She pushed at the pain her words brought. Words she had never dreamed would apply to her and Cassie.

"Besides, it's our second day married.'' She tried to grin. "Seems we should do something together. You know, honeymoon on the water tower sled trail.'' Her attempt at humor failed to lighten his somber mood.

"I have work to do,'' he said quietly.

She lifted her chin slightly. "On Saturday?'' she challenged.

"On Saturday,'' he said firmly.

"It wouldn't hurt for you to get out for a little while.'' She almost added that he had to start living a full life again, move past the darkness of his loss. But he leaned back and spoke before she could formulate the right words.

"I thought that one of the reasons we married was so that Cassie would have someone to care for her while I worked.''

She glared at him, then stood, put her hands on her hips, looking him in the eye. "She doesn't seem to want me to care for her, for reasons beyond me. And just because I'm here, because we're married, doesn't mean you still don't need to spend more time with your daughter,'' Sharon said quietly.

"I know that,'' he said in a low voice. "But I really do need to get this work done.''

Recognizing defeat, she sighed.

"I'll let you off the hook this time,'' she said. Then turned and left him to his work.

Chapter Five

Cassie was in her room, coloring. Brittany curled on the foot of the bed, sleeping. The pup cracked an eye, thumped her tail when Sharon knocked at the open door. Cassie froze, then slowly lifted her eyes to Sharon, red crayon poised above the page.

"It's a nice day for sledding," Sharon said, and saw immediate refusal in Cassie's eyes. "Brittany and I are going. If you'd like to come along, you can." She snapped her fingers and the pup jumped to the floor, tail wagging her whole body as she rushed over to Sharon.

Cassie looked out the window, at Sharon, then at Brittany, clearly torn. "It is totally up to you," Sharon finally said, as if it mattered little to her, when in truth her heart was breaking. "If you want to come along, get your snowsuit on."

Several minutes later she perched on a stepladder in the garage dressed in her snow clothes, sled dug out and dusted off, while Brittany eagerly snuffled around the snow machines. Cassie wasn't coming. Sharon's heart sank. The last thing she wanted was to go sledding by herself. But...

She stood and dusted her snow pants, grabbed the rope of the sled and started to turn. The door into the house opened just a crack. She stopped. It stopped. Then it opened a bit farther. Cassie peered out at her. Silent. Like a wild animal caught in the glare of headlights, wanting to flee yet unable to.

A tiny burst of hope flared in Sharon's chest. She smiled carefully, then said, "Ready? Well, let's go, then." She hurried the dog and little girl out the side door before Cassie could change her mind.

Soon Cassie's laughter rang out, capturing Sharon's heart as no other sound could. And if Cassie hesitated before accepting Sharon's help up after she spilled off the sled and into the snow, that was okay, because she was smiling. And laughing. And the next time the hesitation was less. And the next time she leaned into Sharon for just a few seconds longer than necessary, Sharon pretended not to notice, even as her heart sang. And when she allowed Sharon a quick hug—in fact, returned one of her own—Sharon just knew that things were going to get better.

If only Grant were here, the afternoon would be perfect. One day, she promised herself. But for now she was going to enjoy what she had, and not dwell on anything negative.

They played in the brilliant sunshine and crisp temperatures for well over two hours. Cassie's nose turned red; her eyes flashed with laughter; her cheeks colored a deep pink. When they finally decided to go in, Brittany masqueraded as a snowball tree, huge clumps of snow and ice clinging to every inch of her underside and ears.

Sharon groaned when she took a good look at the pup, and wondered why she didn't get a husky, a dog who shed the snow as easily as a duck shed water. Then Brittany woofed and smiled up at her, bright eyed, curly eared. She dismissed the traitorous thought immediately, reaching to give the pup a quick pat.

They turned back to the house, fingers and toes numb with cold in spite of gloves and boots. And with each step they took, Cassie grew quieter, less animated, like a turtle pulling inside her shell, until nothing remained of the laughing little girl who had so willingly given hugs just minutes earlier.

Sharon's spirits dropped as she watched the metamorphosis. She almost suggested they sled longer, but they couldn't stay outside forever. "Is anything wrong, Cass?" she finally asked.

Cassie hesitated, shot Sharon a quick glance, then looked back down at the ground and shook her head.

"Would you tell me if there was?" Sharon asked, though she wasn't sure she wanted the answer. Cassie hesitated once more, then shrugged without speaking, the non-answer a "No" as clearly as if the word had been spoken. Sharon wished she had not asked, and didn't press the little girl further.

Once inside the garage, Cassie silently helped put the sled away, took off her snowsuit and hung it on a hook on the wall to dry, then headed toward the house door.

Sharon's heart sank somewhere around the depths of her toes. Then the little girl stopped, turned back. Sharon's heart leaped.

"Thank you for taking me sledding," Cassie said quietly, then she turned and went into the house.

A dozen pale-pink roses greeted Sharon in her room, with a card that simply said, *I am sorry,* written in Grant's bold handwriting.

She smiled and touched a delicate flower. The rich scent of the blooms filled the room, lifting her spirits. She shimmied out of her long underwear, took a quick shower, pulled on shapeless sweats and headed for the kitchen, anxious to see Grant.

Cassie sat at the table. Grant stopped in the act of opening a cardboard box from the Chinese-food restaurant. His eyes as they captured hers were dark, inscrutable. Unsmiling and unnaturally still. She wanted to walk across the room into his arms. Her heart jumped at the thought. She dismissed it, smiled and swept by him to the fridge. "Soda, anyone?"

She gathered three cans, set them on the table, then leaned against Grant's shoulder, ignoring the sudden surge of her pulse. "I owe you an apology, also, for pushing too hard. But we won't argue about that, okay? Apology accepted," she said softly. "And the flowers are beautiful. Not necessary, but beautiful nonetheless."

The food was excellent, the kitchen filled with Cassie's chatter as she regaled Grant with sledding incidents and the exploits of Brittany. Sharon ate slowly, savoring the few minutes of emotional peace. She was not going to think about anything at the moment, just savor. And she did.

When Grant and Cassie started clearing the table, she shooed them away. "You picked up dinner," she told Grant, "I'll clean up."

"Such a deal." He smiled, a crooked smile that caught at her heart.

"Well, you're not being let off that easy," she teased. "Go build a fire."

Two hours later, they all sprawled in the family room. Logs popped and snapped in the heat of the flames. Soft music from the stereo rose and fell in gentle swells. Cassie lay on her stomach on the floor, reading a book, Brittany at her side. The little girl enunciated each word carefully so that the pup could hear, oblivious to Brittany's snores.

Grant stretched on the sofa, face turned toward the fire. Sharon curled beneath a blanket on the love seat. Every bone and muscle in her body ached. Too much sledding and cold for a body used to sitting behind a desk.

She stretched and groaned. Grant and Cassie looked at her. "I think I might have overdone it today." She threw the blanket back and slowly sat up, wincing. "I'd better go to bed early. I'm feeling a little under the weather and need all the beauty sleep I can get."

"See you in the morning," Grant said. Cassie just watched silently as Sharon left the room.

Sharon dreamed that she was in a rose garden; the sweet scent of flowers filled the air. Grant walked toward her, a smile on his face. Her heart pounded in double time, and she forced herself not to run toward him. He drew closer, the warmth of his smile washing over her. The welcoming smile of a lover. A familiar, unspoken invitation. Her breath caught. He reached out to take her hand; their fingers instantly intertwined as if they had done it a million times before. He pulled her to him, head lowering until their lips were fractions of an inch apart. Their breath intermingled; their lips started to touch.

And then Grant screamed.

A heart-stopping, ear-shattering scream. Sharon jerked upright, heart slamming in her chest as another scream split the air.

Cassie! Sharon leaped from the bed, running the second her feet hit the floor, not bothering with a robe. Grant, clad only in pajama bottoms, had Cassie cradled in his arms, face pressed to his bare chest, her sobs muffled.

His eyes were dark, glittering, his face taut with anguish. Sharon settled next to him on the bed, slid an arm around his waist in a hug of comfort. She ignored the sudden jerk of her pulse. Ignored the heat of his smooth skin against her arm, her hand, the warmth that seeped into her body as they sat, thigh to thigh, shoulder to shoulder.

She reached across him to clasp Cassie's shoulder. "Cass," she half whispered. "It's okay. We're here."

Cassie jerked from her with a screech. "Go away," she howled.

Each word was a vicious stab to Sharon's heart. She gasped and pulled back as if burned. Grant swore.

Cassie struggled to free herself from his arms, eyes wild, tears pouring down her cheeks. "Go away," she cried once more. "I don't want you for my mama. My mama is dead—"

"Cassie!" Grant dragged her back into his arms. "Stop this right—"

Cassie screamed again, an unearthly howl filled with pain and anguish. With unspeakable horror. Sharon's blood turned cold. And then the girl whirled toward her, out of Grant's arms, swinging her arms and fists.

They fell back across the bed together. Sharon tried, but couldn't capture the flying arms, the fists. Brittany barked. Grant swore, then flung himself on top of Cassie and Sharon, flattening Sharon against the mattress. Holding Cassie between them. Arms keeping them secure.

Unexpectedly, Cassie lay as still as a stone, the silence shattering.

Grant met Sharon's eyes, breath warming her cheek, face inches from hers. And then Cassie stirred before either of them could speak.

"I don't want you to die," she moaned. "I'll be good—I will."

Sharon froze. Grant froze. Their gazes locked, their mouths open. A mirror of each other's astonishment. Then Grant rolled to one side until he lay stretched beside them, Cassie still sprawled on top of Sharon. Her arms had somehow wound around Sharon's neck in a grip so tight Sharon had to reach up with trembling hands and loosen it a bit.

Sharon settled her arms around Cassie in a loose hug. Grant dropped his hand on Cassie's shoulder in a clasp of comfort.

"Cassie, just because Sharon is your stepmother now doesn't mean she's going to die. Is that what you think?"

His voice was low, and tugged at Sharon with its gentle tone.

Cassie didn't answer. The only thing moving was her heart beating against Sharon's chest. Then she slowly nodded. Sharon felt her own heart shatter.

"Oh, Cass," she murmured, tightening the hug. "Why didn't you say something?"

The little girl shrugged. Then she slowly raised herself to look Sharon in the eye. "You said you were sick. You were sick and you went to bed because of it." Tears filled her eyes.

"Just sore muscles, little goose. From being outside and getting too chilled," Sharon whispered past the lump in her throat.

"Oh." Cassie straightened farther until she sat in the curve of Grant's arms. "When Mama got sick, I told God that I would be the very best girl...if only she could get better." Her voice trembled. Her lower lip quivered. "I wasn't good enough cause—"

"No." Grant sat up as he growled the word, pulling her around to face him. His eyes glittered in a face devoid of color. "You did *not* cause your mother to die. Do you understand me? Do you?" He was nearly shouting, and gave the little girl a shake when she just gaped at him, eyes wide.

"Grant." Sharon sat up and placed a calming hand on his shoulder. He ignored her.

"You did not cause your mother to die, do you understand? You are not to blame, Cass." He took a deep breath, then said more calmly, "And Sharon is not going to get sick and die because she's your stepmother. Sharon will be fine."

Cassie sat frozen in his grip.

"Do you understand?" he asked hoarsely.

Cassie closed her mouth and finally nodded. His shoulder relaxed just a bit beneath Sharon's grip. He took a deep breath. "And do you believe me?" he then asked quietly.

Sharon's breath caught as the little girl's eyes rounded farther, darkened, remained locked with Grant's. Then she nodded once more and slumped against him as if exhausted.

They sat, silent, for several minutes, until Cassie's breathing evened out and her eyes fluttered shut against her cheeks.

"We need to put her down," Grant said thickly.

Sharon carefully stood, watching as Grant eased Cassie into bed. Lamplight played across the smooth muscle in his back and washed across his broad shoulders as he pulled the blankets up. Her breath caught as his muscle flexed and relaxed, as the light seemed to caress his supple skin. Skin that was hot and hard to the touch. That—

She whirled, slamming a halt to her thoughts. Her cheeks burned, and her hands trembled so badly she clasped them together to keep them still. She did not want to feel this way, her mind screamed. Her body ignored it. The lamp clicked off, throwing the room into sudden darkness and an abrupt, unwelcome intimacy. She barely resisted the urge to forget dignity and run.

"Shall we?" Grant paused by her side. She couldn't look up, could not answer; could only walk quietly out into the hall. Then she forced herself to turn and face him. Forced her gaze to remain on his face and herself to act as if her heart were not pounding so loud she could hardly hear.

Grant closed Cassie's door and leaned against the hall wall with a sigh. He dragged a large hand through his hair, tousling it. Sharon could almost feel the silken strands and ached to mirror the action. She swallowed hard.

Slowly, in spite of her resolve, her eyes dropped to his chest. To the flat muscle covered with thick, dark hair. The lean waist, pajamas that hung on his hips and—

She jerked her gaze back up, heart pounding even louder, so loud she was amazed Grant did not say anything. He didn't. In fact, he hardly even looked at her, choosing instead to focus his attention on the floor.

"I should have known."

His voice was so low she almost couldn't hear the words. When he met her gaze, his eyes were dark and full of self-blame, the muscle in his jaw rigid.

"You've been busy, Grant. Traveling. You can't—"

"Blame anyone but myself." His eyes grew bleak.

"No," Sharon cried softly. "You can't expect to know every thought that Cassie has. Every fear. That is not humanly possible."

Grant didn't answer. Instead, he stood and walked down the hall toward the den without looking at Sharon. Without saying another word.

Sharon hesitated. She should let him go, let him have his privacy. Yet…the memory of his bleak eyes tore at her heart. She had to go and try to help him. She took a deep breath, then walked after Grant.

Grant knew the minute Sharon entered the den.

"Grant?"

Her soft voice wound around him, tightening the knot in his gut. He did not turn to face her.

"Please, leave me alone," he said in a husky voice.

"No," she said quietly. "I think we should talk."

"We don't need to talk," he said as evenly as he could.

She touched his shoulder. He whirled to face her, self-contempt and anger surging through his veins. He didn't stop to analyze as every feeling he had suppressed over the past few years unexpectedly came to life. A roaring tide of irrational emotion that cut through his carefully honed control like a hot knife through butter.

"What is it exactly that you think we have to talk about?" he nearly spit the words. He took a step closer. She tilted her chin, didn't move. They were but inches apart. "The fact that no matter how hard I work, I am failing my daughter?"

"Work? What does work have to do with this?" Sharon interrupted.

He continued as if she hadn't spoken. "No matter how hard I try, it isn't enough. No matter what I do. Maybe Hugh and Dorothy were right. Maybe Cassie would be better off—"

"No," Sharon cried. "I know you don't believe that any more than I do."

"Sometimes I'm not sure what I know. And wasn't it you who said I was working too many hours, that you weren't sure I could raise Cassie on my own?"

"Yes, I did. But I never, not even once, hinted that you were not a good father. Never."

His chest ached as if it were being crushed by a giant fist. They were almost nose to nose. He could feel the heat from her body. Smell the freshness of her shampoo. A hint of lingering perfume.

He wanted to take her, bury his hands in her hair, lose himself in the sudden need that consumed him. A need he did not understand, did not want and that was totally inappropriate. He took a quick step back and whirled away from her. The bitter metallic taste of fear filled his mouth as he struggled for control of the emotions that roiled in his stomach, that screamed for release in his brain.

"Go to bed, Sharon," he said through clenched teeth.

"No. Not as long as you are blaming yourself for something out of your control. Grant, you cannot know Cassie's every thought. Her every fear or insecurity," she said quietly. She placed a hand in the middle of his back.

Her touch left an imprint of warmth between his shoulder blades. "I sure as hell should." His voice was raspy.

"Who appointed you God?" she asked.

Her hand remained as if holding him up. He should have stepped away, walked out of the room. He couldn't.

"No parent could be that omniscient. Why are you expecting that of yourself, Grant?"

She stepped around so that they were facing once again. Grant did not want to meet her gaze but couldn't help himself. Her brown eyes were steady and certain, imploring him to listen, to believe.

"Cassie is a very lucky little girl to have a father who loves her so much. She's lucky to have *you* as her father," she said quietly. When he started to protest, she pressed a finger to his lips. "She is," she insisted.

She reached up to press a kiss to his cheek. A feather-light touch of lips that seized his throat like an iron-clad grip. The words he wanted to utter froze. She stepped back.

"None of us is perfect, Grant. Don't take on more than is humanly possible. You'll only set yourself up for failure, not because you aren't capable but because you're asking the impossible of yourself."

She turned and left the room.

Grant wanted to follow, to grab her arm and argue that she didn't know what she was talking about. Instead, he remained standing, her words reverberating through his mind. He knew she meant every one. And each word, along with her touch, her kiss, was indelibly branded in his mind.

Sharon trembled as the memory of Grant's words, his voice, followed her to bed like a bad dream. She slipped beneath the quilt, aching to help him, wondering if she could.

No matter how hard I work, I am failing my daughter.

Did that explain the long hours? Was Grant driven by an impossible need to provide proof that he loved his daughter? To prove that he was a good father? Although she'd assumed that grief drove Grant to bury himself in work, she now wondered if it wasn't more. Perhaps a combination of grief and an insatiable need to provide for Cassie. Not easy things to shake.

She slowly turned the thoughts in her mind, remembering the tiny trailer Grant had grown up in. The threadbare carpet, linoleum long past a shine, the collection of battered furniture, the secondhand clothes. Sharon had read accounts of incredibly rich men, risen from rags to riches, who could never overcome that legacy of poverty.

She sighed, then turned and buried her face in her pillow. Whatever his reasons, she wanted nothing more than to help Grant.

Sunday turned out to be a peaceful day. They all slept in, then went out for breakfast. While Cassie was still not her old self, she insisted on helping Sharon bake another batch of cookies. Grant spent most of the day in his den, buried in work.

Not perfect, but improvement enough that Sharon went to bed with a heart filled once more with hope.

On Monday morning she beat Grant and Cassie to the kitchen. She let Brittany out and started coffee. She let the pup back in, then turned toward the cupboards to get the oatmeal.

Cassie stood in the doorway, silent, watching, pajama top slipping off one shoulder, face still washed with sleep. Her long hair looked like a haystack after a windstorm.

"Can you fix my hair, Sharon?" she asked uncertainly. "Daddy doesn't do it as good as you."

Sharon's heart flooded with love at the simple request. At the fact that Cassie was standing there, asking. She swallowed a small lump in her throat.

"Of course your daddy doesn't do it as good as me, little goose. I think he has ten thumbs." She walked over to Cassie. The little girl hesitated, then reached up and took her hand. The small fingers seemed to wrap around Sharon's heart, as well.

"I wanta French braid," Cassie said.

"We can handle that," Sharon responded with a smile as they started for the bathroom. "Did I ever tell you about the time your daddy decided to give me a haircut?"

"Yeah." Cassie laughed. "But tell me again, Sharon. Please."

Sharon paused when Grant approached. "Good morning," she said softly. He looked as if he had run a couple of marathons during the night. Dark eyes shadowed. Face drawn. She resisted the impulse to step closer, to cup his jaw in her hand. Her stomach fluttered at the thought.

His gaze captured her, held her in one spot. For a minute, she thought he would pass without speaking. "Cassie, you go on. I'll be right with you," she said. Cassie raced down the hall into the bathroom.

"I'm running late for an early meeting. I'll have to skip breakfast this morning," Grant said. He started to walk by.

Sharon took a deep breath to calm a sudden dance of nerves, then said, "Can we talk just a minute?"

He stopped, back and shoulders stiff. She made it easier for him by walking around to face him. Their gazes met, hers searching, his careful. "I...something you said the other night made me wonder..."

His eyes narrowed as if resisting the reminder of their conversation on Saturday. She ignored the silent warning and spoke anyway. "Grant, being a good father doesn't necessarily mean an overflowing toy box. Or dressers and closets jam-packed with clothes."

His jaw tightened. She squared her shoulders. "What I mean is...well, you don't have to work so hard all the time. You don't have anything to prove to anyone. You are a good father, Grant, in spite of the hours you work."

He arched a brow. She flushed as a wave of heat washed her face. "I mean...meant...that did not—"

"I think I know what you meant and I appreciate your concern. But I work the hours I do because the job demands it," he said quietly, then he turned and walked off.

The scent of his aftershave lingered, bringing images to mind that she had no business entertaining.

Grant had trouble concentrating in his first meeting as snippets of what Sharon had said that morning, of their conversation from Saturday night, kept popping to mind. Unbidden, disconcerting as they interrupted his flow of thought, his concentration.

You are a good father, Grant, in spite of the hours you work.

Compliment or backhanded criticism? Except, he knew that Sharon meant the words as a compliment. If she wanted to criticize, she would.

He was late to a second meeting.

Cassie is a very lucky little girl to have a father who loves her so much. She's lucky to have you *as her father.*

He wanted to believe those words, did for the most part. But there were moments when he would be clutched by a fist of uncertainty, of fear that he was not doing enough. He nearly forgot a third meeting.

Being a good father doesn't necessarily mean an overflowing toy box. Or dressers and closets jam-packed with clothes.

He knew that, but those things were a part of being a good parent, he silently argued. And he wasn't sure he liked what Sharon was implying. A few days ago, she accused him of hiding from grief by working so much. And now...now she was implying he worked because of Cassie. Which he did, but...

His thoughts slowly circled, gaining strength as they fed on one another. Ricocheted from one to another. He did work to provide for Cassie, and that was an important part of being a parent, at least for him. But was there more? Was he burying himself in his work to avoid something? Certainly not to escape grief. Certainly to provide. But was it necessary to work the hours he worked?

The thought gave pause, and suddenly he was filled with a maelstrom of doubt. His heart beat harder than normal, and his throat dried. He was flooded with memories of times when he had pushed other questions back, worked harder, coming home too exhausted to do more than deal with Cassie. Never time to—

He slammed a halt to his thoughts, overwhelmed. He was making more out of this than there was. Or was he? The phone rang. By the time he finished the conversation, he had pushed all thoughts out of his mind except for what pertained to work. Each time other concerns tried to resurface, he firmly squashed them. Later, he told himself, when he had more time.

By the end of the week, he still hadn't found the time.

Chapter Six

Gray clouds hovered over Valdez Saturday morning, heavy with the threat of snow, dampening spirits in spite of the bright kitchen lights. Bacon sputtered in the pan, filling the kitchen with its scent. Grant deftly turned the pieces, while Cassie set the table.

"I wanta do something," Cassie grumbled.

"You are," he answered.

"Daddy! I mean something fun," she complained as she rolled her eyes. "Can we go sledding, Sharon?"

Sharon paused in the act of buttering toast, glancing at Cassie and then Grant. "Cass, I'm sorry, but I can't. I have to go into work for a few hours this morning. Maybe when I get back."

"Work? On a Saturday?" Grant arched a brow and pretended astonishment. Sharon stuck out her tongue. He couldn't help but grin, a finger of warmth tickling through him.

"Sharon's gonna work. Daddy's gonna work." Cassie's lower lip stuck out. "What are Brittany and me gonna do for fun?"

He started to say that he *had* to work, then glanced down at Cassie. She looked like a poster child for neglected children, eyes wide and begging. A fist of guilt clutched his gut. Sharon cleared her throat and shot a pointed look that stabbed his conscience.

She didn't need to say that she thought he worked too much. She didn't need to say that she thought he should spend more time having fun, playing with Cassie. Because she had already said all those things.

He *could* rightfully argue that he should work. That what he had brought home in his briefcase was a small portion of what actually needed his attention. He opened his mouth to say so, when Brittany whined. He looked down into a pair of sad spaniel eyes, then over once again at a woebegone Cassie. Sharon cleared her throat once more, and Grant admitted defeat.

Sharon was right. It wouldn't hurt to take the day off. He could always work tomorrow.

"How about if we all go cross-country skiing when Sharon gets back?" Grant asked slowly. Their mouths dropped open. He scowled. "You can quit acting like I just suggested we barbecue Brittany for lunch."

"Daddy!" Cassie giggled, eyes bright. "Can we really go skiing? You'll go with us?"

Her cheeks pinkened when he nodded. Guilt stabbed at him again at her obvious excitement.

Sharon was right. He hadn't been spending enough time playing with his daughter, and he suddenly felt like the world's worst father.

"Yeah, really," he said gruffly.

Cassie cheered. Brittany yelped. Sharon smiled; a slow, warm smile that twisted around him like a soft caress.

"Excellent idea," she said.

Her tone of voice somehow made him feel about ten

feet tall. And a fool for feeling that way, because he did not deserve it.

Cassie and Brittany helped him dig out the skis and poles, the little girl chattering nonstop and the dog constantly underfoot. After the third time of nearly killing himself tripping over one or the other, he sent both of them to Cassie's room with orders to search for warm clothing. Sharon returned just as he finished waxing the skis. She hurried and changed her clothes.

"I thought we'd drive down to the dike road by Mineral Creek," he said as Sharon, Cassie and a wiggling Brittany piled into the pickup with a flurry of color and motion. Cassie squeezed next to Sharon; Brittany squashed between her and Grant.

For just a minute, Grant wished that it were Sharon squashed against him, the warmth of her body burning into his. He frowned and pushed the thought away, focusing instead on the excitement and high spirits that filled the pickup cab.

Snow started to spit from the sky; light, tiny flakes that gently floated through the air. An eagle soared overhead, head and tail brilliant white against the gray sky.

When they got to the trail and were preparing their gear, Grant started to instruct Cassie how to ski. She protested with an indignant scowl that she knew how to ski from her vast experience two years earlier—a sum total of two trips, which Grant was surprised she even remembered. He fought a grin as she put her hands on her hips and frowned at him.

"Those were different skis. You need to let me show you how to use these new skis that Sharon and Santa got for you," he explained.

Cassie chewed her lower lip, thinking. "Okay," she finally decided. "But can you please hurry? Brittany and me wanta go." The pup danced at her side as if to strengthen the child's argument.

Grant arched a brow at Sharon. She winked and smiled, a slow curve of lips that washed warmth through his body.

Disturbed by the reaction, he quickly returned his attention to Cassie. It was nothing but his imagination, he told himself. He helped his daughter with her skis until she finally insisted with a "Daddy!" that she was ready to do it on her own.

Grant shook his head and stepped back to watch his daughter clamber down the trail with quick, jerky strides. She fell with a shriek. Brittany dove to lick her face. They scrambled up together before Grant could go to the rescue. Instead of tears, laughter spilled from Cassie.

"She's just like you were at that age," Sharon said with a gentle laugh.

The sound wound around him like a soft rope and pulled. He resisted and continued to watch Cassie. She fell again with a scream that turned to sputtered laughter. Up she climbed, arms and legs flailing and pumping furiously as she struggled down the trail.

"At the rate she's going, she'll be so pooped by the time we get to the bend we'll have to go home," Sharon said softly.

Grant slowly turned toward her, oddly reluctant to face her and disturbed by that reluctance. Cold kissed her cheeks and nose pink. Her eyes sparkled between thick, brown lashes. Burnished curls spilled from beneath a rust-colored stocking hat, forming a soft frame for her face. His pulse skipped a beat. He almost reached to touch her cheek; had his hand half-raised, when he realized what he was doing and jerked back, grabbed both ski poles firmly and turned. "Ready?" He strode forward, not waiting for an answer.

Running? No, he denied. He had nothing to run from.

An image of Sharon's flushed face came to mind. He pushed it away and concentrated on his skis as they slid smoothly through the snow. He could blame the sudden pound of heart on the unaccustomed exercise.

The fresh air was cold and clean and filled with Cassie's laughter, a bark from Brittany, a raspy *caw-caw* of a raven perched in the naked branches of a cottonwood tree.

He sucked in a lungful of air, enjoying the crisp cold. Enjoying the rush of blood, the *swoosh-swoosh* of Sharon's skis as she easily kept pace at his side.

Muscles unused to physical activity protested. Yet...it felt good. Right. Old feelings long buried slowly started to surface, and with them the sense of pleasure he had always gotten from being outside. From pushing himself physically. How long had it been since he'd enjoyed the simple pleasures in life? When had he stopped doing the things he loved, and why? Because Catherine hated them? Or because he had quit caring, buried as he always was beneath a pile of never-ending work?

Was Sharon just a bit right? Did he use work to avoid dealing with some of the issues in his life?

Nonsense, he silently argued, but the denial didn't have quite the conviction it used to.

Cassie stopped at the sloping curve that led into the riverbed, Grant and Sharon pausing on each side of her. "This is fun!"

She was panting, cheeks a bright red. Her teeth shone like tiny white pearls when she flashed a smile. Then she shot down the hill before Grant could issue his words of caution.

Sharon laughed, drawing his gaze. "I'm telling you, Grant, she's so much like you at that age it's almost spooky." Her smile dimmed, then died, replaced by a pensive frown.

Grant did not need to ask what she was thinking. He knew.

Sharon would never have a daughter who looked or acted like her, who carried her blood, smiled her smile, shared the same rich red-brown of her hair. Because she had married him.

A knot of guilt twisted his stomach.

She was not going to have children anyway, had not planned to marry, he reminded himself.

Somehow the thought did not make him feel much better.

"Let's catch up," she said, then took off.

Her slender hips held his gaze, until he jerked his eyes away with a frown. He put his head down and followed, concentrating only on his skis. On the furious strides that carried him down the trail as if they would carry him away from the disturbing questions and thoughts that he suddenly could not seem to control.

Cassie screamed with laughter. Brittany barked. Grant looked up just in time to see Sharon struggling to climb to her feet on the trail smack in front of him. She almost made it. He did not have time to stop. Had no room to step around. She half turned to face him, eyes wide. His ski caught hers, and they catapulted to the ground. Landed with a thud, Sharon squashed beneath Grant.

Hip to hip. Chest to chest. Her breath warmed his neck. Impressions of soft curves all in the right places rushed to mind. Desire slammed through him, so fast and unexpected he nearly gasped. He jumped up and away, toes screaming in pain as they twisted in his bindings. He tripped sideways, nearly stabbed himself with Sharon's ski pole, and landed face first in the snow. No soft curves to cushion the fall. Nothing but bitter cold snow that had him catching his breath, and a branch that poked him in the ribs.

Thoughts whirled through his mind like snowflakes in a

blizzard. He couldn't be attracted to Sharon. Not like that! She was his best friend, damn it.

"Grant? Are you okay?"

Sharon's gentle voice filled with concern shivered along his spine like a finger tracing against bare skin, bringing another rush of desire. Another flood of unwanted images.

He squeezed his eyes shut and swallowed a groan. "Yeah, I am just fine." Slowly levering himself off the ground, he was careful not to look at her as if she might be able to read his thoughts.

It was nothing, he told himself as he stood and brushed snow from his body. Just a momentary reaction to unexpected physical contact. And then he tried his hardest to make himself believe it.

The day finally caught up with Cassie halfway through the dinner they enjoyed at a small local restaurant. Her eyes began to droop and her chin hovered a bit too close to the table. Sharon arched a brow and smiled at him. Grant smiled back and fought to ignore the inviting curve of her lips, the softness in her eyes and the way freckles sprinkled like fairy kisses across her nose and cheeks.

Best friend, he reminded himself. Yet the sudden tension that shimmered through him had absolutely nothing to do with friendship.

Cassie fell asleep a few blocks from the restaurant. The trip home was made in silence. A silence even heavier once the garage door growled closed behind them and the pickup engine cut.

"I'll put her in bed," Grant whispered, then scooped her in his arms, following Sharon as she opened the door.

Brittany greeted them with excited bounces, and Sharon took the pup outside while Grant carried his sleeping daughter to bed.

By the time he'd threaded limp arms into the sleeves of

a flannel nightgown and tucked her in, Sharon was in the family room, a fire started. She had changed from jeans and a sweatshirt to a large T-shirt and leggings.

She crouched in front of the fireplace, hands held out to the flames; when he walked into the room she rose and turned. Firelight rose with her, outlining and bathing the contours of her body in a caress that started at her slender hips and climbed upward, accentuating each and every curve.

He jerked his eyes to her face, heart suddenly pounding harder than normal, throat dry. "She's asleep," he said in a husky voice, then quickly cleared his throat.

"She had fun. We need to get out more."

Sharon smiled, the curve of her lips making his blood race.

"Thanks for today," she continued. "I know you could have worked, but it really meant a lot to Cassie to get out, to spend the day with you. And I enjoyed it, as well."

Her words tugged at something deep inside, as unsettling as the physical desire he battled.

"I had fun, too," he finally managed.

A log popped and flames flickered. Like a finely tuned antenna, he knew without looking when Sharon moved. Could almost hear her breathing, and had to force himself not to look, not to watch as the firelight danced around her.

He fought the images that the mere thought brought. The room was warm and suddenly far too small. And Grant knew he could not remain a minute longer.

"Think I'll turn in early," he said hoarsely. He met her gaze, ignored the puzzlement in her eyes, because the last thing he was going to do was explain that he couldn't stay in the room with her. That somehow, his libido had gotten out of control and all his energy was directed at her.

It was only natural, he supposed. Two healthy adults, in

their prime, thrown together in a very emotional situation. It wasn't that he *really* wanted Sharon.

Ha! a tiny voice shouted.

He didn't, he told himself firmly, then turned and walked from the room. Heading straight for the coldest shower he could stand.

Cassie and Grant were in the kitchen, their voices drifting to Sharon as she neared the door. Cassie giggled. Grant said something, his voice a murmur. Longing spread through Sharon at the sound, but she quickly dismissed it.

Grant was her friend, nothing more, and she was not going to risk that friendship by letting this silly attraction be more than what it was. Unwanted and fleeting. Given time, she was certain it would die a natural death. Meanwhile, she was going to steadfastly ignore it.

Cassie sat on the counter next to Grant, who stood, stirring something in a large bowl. Sharon allowed a quick look down the length of his body. Snug T-shirt tucked into faded jeans that hugged his lower body. A sight that any woman would find appealing, she reminded herself when her pulse skittered. A normal reaction and nothing she could not control.

"Good morning," she said, perhaps a shade too brightly.

"'Morning," Grant answered.

He faced her with a smile that tested her resolve, then he turned back to his bowl.

"Daddy and me are makin' an omelet," Cassie said.

Sharon walked over and gathered Cassie in her arms. "Is that right, little goose? Well, I'm sure that if you're helping him it will be delicious." Cassie's arms slowly wound around Sharon's neck in a grip so tight and fierce her heart sang.

"This is good," Sharon said later as she cut into the

omelet for another bite. Rich cheese, chunks of smoky ham and fresh mushrooms spilled onto the plate. "Matter of fact, it's excellent."

Cassie laughed, a sound that made Sharon smile. "I told you so," the little girl said. "Daddy is a good cook."

"Yes, he is," Sharon agreed. "A man of many talents."

She glanced at him. His dark gaze caught and held her. Her heart swelled, then he turned his attention back to his plate.

Cassie finished first, excused herself and went outside with Brittany. Grant pushed back his plate, reached for his mug of coffee.

"Are you going to work today?" Sharon asked.

His eyes met hers over the mug. "Why?"

"Well, I thought... I hoped that maybe we could spend some time together. Maybe go sledding, or skiing again."

He slowly lowered the mug, hesitated, then got up from the table. "I'll have to pass today." He started stacking plates.

"You can't hide in your work forever, Grant. I thought maybe you were beginning to realize that," she said quietly.

He looked at her. "Hide? And here I thought all along that I was doing my job."

Sharon took a deep breath. "You are, of course, but if you're honest with yourself, you'll admit that you're spending far more hours than you have to working." She continued before he could interrupt. "I know it's been hard for you, Grant. But you can't deal with your grief by working—"

"Grief?" he repeated quietly.

Sharon nodded, silenced by his dark gaze.

"Cassie is the reason I work. And the fact that my job requires a lot of hours."

"Cassie is the reason you shouldn't work so many

hours," Sharon said stubbornly. "She needs more of your time, Grant, not more of the things money can buy."

"Are you suggesting I quit my job?"

His voice was soft, too soft, and Sharon recognized suppressed anger.

"No, but—"

"If I'm such a terrible parent, I'm surprised you didn't side with Hugh and Dorothy," he said softly.

"That is not what—"

He walked out of the room without a backward glance.

"That's not what I meant," Sharon said to the empty room. "And you changed the subject," she added, although no one was there to hear.

She wanted to go after him, to urge him to let her help. Because she had never in her life wanted to help someone so badly. It was an ache, a need that went bone deep and penetrated her soul. If only she knew how, knew what to do. And she could not believe that Cassie or job responsibilities were the only reasons he worked the hours he did.

Grant did not believe he was hiding from anything, but driven by Sharon's words, he did make an effort to leave the office earlier the next day, filling his briefcase with paperwork that could be done once Cassie was in bed.

The golden glow of light spilled from the windows to wash across the driveway in welcome as Grant pulled in. The house drew him as it never had before.

Faint giggles greeted him as he opened the door. A sound that brought a smile to his face and lightened his step as he set aside the briefcase and walked through the kitchen into the family room. Brightly colored afghans hung over the backs of the kitchen chairs in an oddly shaped tent. At one corner, Brittany's tail stuck out.

A tail that Brittany wouldn't have had if Sharon hadn't

been outraged when the breeder had told her they would be docking the tails of all the pups just after birth. She was so outraged she'd agreed to buy each and every pup, then and there, if the breeder left their tails intact. Fortunately, the litter was small—five puppies. And Sharon had had no trouble finding four like-minded folks in Valdez for the rest of the pups.

Another volley of giggles brought him back to present. He cleared his throat. "Anyone home?"

"Daddy!" Cassie squealed, and burst from beneath the afghans. "You're home early!" She threw herself at him, nearly knocking him off his feet.

Sharon poked her head from beneath the afghans. "We're having a tea party," she explained. Her cheeks were soft pink, her eyes warm with welcome.

"Ah. I knew that, of course," he said.

"You gotta come, too, Daddy. Please. Please." Cassie dragged at his hand while dancing in front of him. "It's really milk, but we're pretending that it's tea."

"Just for one cup."

Sharon's eyes challenged him, as well as her words. He couldn't refuse the soft lure of her voice any more than he could the tug of Cassie's hand. "Okay, okay," he agreed. Cassie cheered, and Sharon's smile widened, warmed and wrapped around him as if a physical touch. He had to pull his gaze away.

Brittany leaped up and licked his face when he poked it in the tent. He sputtered. Sharon grabbed the pup and laughed. Their gazes caught and held briefly, then he looked at his tiny daughter. Her eyes were sparkling, and his heart swelled with love.

She beamed at both of them as Grant settled, cross-legged, directly across from Sharon. Their knees almost touched, and he had to hunch a bit to fit beneath the sagging roof.

Cassie poured the milk into small teacups, tongue caught between her teeth, a frown of concentration on her brow. She carefully passed a cup to Grant and then one to Sharon, not spilling a drop. Then she filled three small plastic plates with a cookie each and passed them out. She settled back with a grin. "Isn't this fun?" She broke a chunk of cookie off and dunked it in her milk.

He looked at Sharon. She grinned back. "Does this remind you of anything?" he asked, voice low and almost husky.

Her eyes shone with unvoiced laughter. "You couldn't possibly be referring to the time you and your brothers crashed my tea party, could you?"

"Daddy, you didn't?" Cassie cried.

"He most certainly did," Sharon insisted with a smile. "I had six friends over, and he and both your uncles decided to turn their hamsters loose, then shout "Mouse." You have never heard such screaming. Seven little girls shrieking their lungs out. Scared one hamster so bad, he ran and hid and it took a week to find him."

"Daddy!"

Cassie looked scandalized. Grant chuckled, a rumble that seemed to expand when released.

"It's not funny," Cassie argued. "Boy!" She rolled her eyes. "If Johnny did that I would—"

"Better not blacken his eye again," Sharon broke in.

Cassie frowned, then arched a brow. "Even if he really deserved it?"

"Even if he really deserved it," Grant and Sharon said together.

And then the three of them laughed, a melody of friendship that had a smile playing on Sharon's lips even after the sound died.

Soft light filtered into the tent, capturing her in its patterned web. Small squares of light settled on her skin.

Grant's gaze stopped on her lips. Tender, kissable lips. He realized with a sense of resignation that he wanted to kiss them, to taste them. And though the eyes that looked so warmly at him were eyes he'd seen a million times, they weren't the same. They were the eyes of a woman, rich and mysterious, full of promise.

Sharon was no longer the little girl next door, the sister he'd never had. She'd grown into an attractive woman he ached to take into his arms, if only for the moment. Grant suddenly wished that they were alone in the thick dusk of the tent. That his fingers were dancing across her skin. Instead, his fingers tightened around the small plastic cup.

"I gotta go get more cookies." Cassie shot from the tent, Brittany racing after.

"Those two are nearly inseparable." Sharon's gaze locked with his and held. The laughter slowly died. "What is it?" she asked. "Do I have cookie on my face?" She reached a hand upward, and he captured it without volition.

He knew better.

Her eyes widened.

He should stop now. Pull back before he did something they both regretted. He couldn't.

Her lips parted as he dipped his head. Surprise or invitation? He didn't stop to answer the question, just leaned closer until her eyes fluttered shut and his lips settled against hers like a sigh.

Soft, gentle, slowly deepening as need grew. Until need threatened to take over and Grant, barely able to, pulled back. Sharon stared at him, cheeks flushed a deep pink, lips trembling, eyes wide. A woman who had been thoroughly kissed by a man who'd thoroughly enjoyed it.

"I'm sorry. I shouldn't have done that," he said in a husky voice.

He shouldn't want to do it again, either. He was the biggest heel in the world for taking advantage of a friend to begin with, then wanting more.

Chapter Seven

Sharon could only stare at Grant. He flushed. "Sharon, I—"

"No." She almost cried the word. "It's okay, Grant." She couldn't bear another apology. Not while the feel, the taste, of his lips still clung to hers. Not when her heart galloped wildly, racing her pulse. Not while she ached, ached until it hurt, to lean forward and repeat the very action he so clearly regretted.

An action she should also regret.

"But—"

"There is no need to apologize, no need to make a big deal out of nothing," she said firmly.

His eyes narrowed. "Nothing—"

"I'm back," Cassie sang out, stopping Grant's angry growl. The little girl scrambled into the tent with a fistful of cookies, Brittany at her heels.

"Nothing," Sharon repeated softly.

The muscle in his jaw tightened. He opened his mouth, then slowly closed it and nodded. A quick nod, acknowledging acquiescence.

He didn't need to agree quite so quickly.

Don't be ridiculous, Sharon told herself, and dismissed the thought.

There is no need to apologize, no need to make a big deal out of nothing.

Nothing! Grant muttered an oath and paced the length of the bedroom, unable to sleep, unable to erase the memory of what Sharon had so blithely referred to as "nothing."

It didn't help that she was right. It was only a kiss. Yet...

His steps slowed as he glared at the bed as if it were somehow responsible for the images that kept coming to mind. Images he had no business entertaining when it came to Sharon. She had married him, trusting that there would be no physical aspect to the relationship.

That was the way he wanted it, damn it.

It was, he told himself for about the millionth time. It did not matter that Sharon was an attractive woman. She didn't look any different from the way she'd looked before they had married, so why did he suddenly find her so appealing?

He dropped to the bed and buried his face in his hands with a groan. He didn't know. Did not understand. And the worst of it was, he was not sure his attraction to her was going to go away all that easily.

They could consummate the relationship.

His heart skipped a beat at the thought, and just as quickly he dismissed the idea. He couldn't suggest that to Sharon. She was his friend, and the last thing he wanted was to take advantage.

Unless she happened to agree.

He snorted. Yeah, right. And pigs could fly.

He flopped back to stare at the ceiling. He was married

to a woman he suddenly wanted so bad it hurt, and he would never touch her. It was the honorable thing to do because he could never offer her more than a physical relationship.

He could never offer her love.

The next morning, Grant acted as if nothing had happened. Sharon wasn't sure whether she should be offended or relieved. And she couldn't help but wonder if maybe she had read more into the situation than was there.

It had been, after all, only a kiss. Something they had shared as casually as hugs their entire friendship.

Not that kind of kiss, a tiny voice argued.

She was determined to ignore it.

Grant worked late that night. Sharon and Cassie ate a quick dinner, then Cassie took Brittany out into the yard to play. Restless, Sharon tried to read, but gave up two pages and twenty minutes later. The house didn't need cleaning because they had someone come in once a week to do it. Things were running smoothly at the office, so she couldn't distract herself with work. And she was not in the mood to go outside in the chill of night and roll around in the snow with Cassie and Brittany.

She wanted Grant to come home.

Of course she did, she told herself. Because he was her friend. There couldn't be more to it than that. She had learned years ago there was no point in walking down that path. She was nothing more to Grant than a friend who was helping him out.

And that was all she wanted, she reminded herself. One time, she had wanted more, much more. But now, even if Grant was interested, she had nothing to offer.

Restlessness surged through her. She leaped to her feet as if fleeing her thoughts, walked down to her room and stood surveying it with a frown. Then she walked over and grabbed the box of throw pillows. It was ridiculous to have them shoved in a box when they could be used. She scattered them in colorful disarray on couches and chairs throughout the house. If Grant disapproved, he could say so.

If he noticed, he didn't say a word. He smiled a weary smile as they passed in the hall just after Sharon had tucked Cassie and Brittany into bed, then he turned into Cassie's room, and Sharon didn't see him until the next morning at breakfast, when he silently ate a quick bowl of cereal, then sped off for an early meeting.

That evening, Cassie brought home a couple of small finger paintings she had made at day care. Their bright, bold colors and simple shapes had such appeal and Cassie was so obviously proud of them that Sharon drove down to the drugstore and bought frames before starting dinner. Cassie helped her hang the paintings in the family room.

Sharon clapped her hands. "Perfect." She knelt and gave Cassie a hug. "They are perfect."

The little girl's face glowed. There was no other word to describe the wide grin, pink cheeks and shining eyes. Cassie dragged Grant through the kitchen and into the family room that night to show him before he'd hardly had a chance to say hello.

Sharon was pulling baked chicken from the oven when he returned alone. She set it on top of the stove and turned back to making a salad. He settled against the counter, not speaking.

"Well?" Sharon finally asked, chopping tomatoes with quick slices of the knife. She nearly screamed when Grant placed a hand on her arm, startling her. She slowly turned to face him, heart pounding. His hand fell away, but not the memory of its imprint against her bare skin.

"That was a very nice thing to do," he said quietly.

She tried to shrug off the warm pleasure his words gave. "It's something anyone would—"

"No, it isn't. Anyone would have tacked them to the fridge with a magnet. You're a good mother to her."

His dark eyes traveled across her face like a physical touch. Her pulse surged. She fought to control it.

"She was so very proud of them I thought a little special effort was in order. And I thought we could replace the artwork from time to time with something new she's made and keep a scrapbook of the outdated things," she said, voice husky. She cleared her throat and resisted the urge to step forward, closer to Grant. A nameless want welled up from within. An ache she didn't understand and wasn't sure she wanted to survey too closely because it seemed more than simple desire.

His dark eyes held her like an embrace, causing a shiver to race the length of her body. Drawing an awareness of herself as a woman, with wants and needs that only—

"When's dinner?" Cassie trotted into the kitchen, Brittany at her side.

Sharon pulled around to finish the salad. Her hands shook so bad she hoped she wouldn't slice the end of a finger off. "In just a minute," she answered, relieved that her voice didn't tremble, also.

She refused to complete the thought that Cassie had interrupted. There was no point walking a dead-end trail.

Grant flew to Anchorage on the morning flight the next day, planning to return the following afternoon. By evening, clouds had settled over the mountains and snow fell in thick, steady waves. The muffled roar of snowblowers drifted to Sharon from the Mineral Creek subdivision below as she stood on the deck.

With Cassie and Brittany in bed, Sharon was once again filled with restless energy. Laundry was caught up, still warm from the dryer and folded. The cookie jar was full.

She rarely turned television on, and wasn't in the mood to be frightened out of her wits by the newest thriller she had bought at the drugstore.

So she hunched her shoulders against the cold, lifted her face to let it be bathed by snowflakes and told herself that her restlessness had nothing to do with the fact that she missed Grant.

Liar, her conscience charged.

She didn't argue. With him gone, the house seemed... too empty. Not that it meant anything, she told herself with a frown. Just that she had grown used to having him around. And she did not need to make more of it than that.

So she pushed the thought aside, went back into the house and wandered from room to room. She stopped in the living room to study the prints on the walls. She had seen bolder, more original work while visiting the day care. These contained streaks and splashes of color in matching metal frames, without meaning or merit other than to go with the color decor of the room in which they hung. She would not hang them in her bathroom.

Were these prints that Grant had chosen with Catherine? Prints that he liked? She could hardly believe it, hardly believe that the vital, alive Grant she used to know would want something so...lifeless.

But, then, the Grant she was married to little resembled the boy she had watched grow into a young man. A young man who'd spent as much time outdoors as in. Who had laughed and smiled more often than not, able to enjoy life and have fun. He was so much different from the serious, office-bound Grant, who seemed to live only for Cassie and work, that Sharon wanted to cry.

Crying was a waste of time. She glared at the prints once more; the prints in the bottom of her closet seemed to scream out to her, suffocating, begging escape from their dark prison. She gnawed her bottom lip, torn. Grant did say he didn't care what she did around the house. And he had not minded the battered bookshelves she had dragged into the family room, with their worn paperbacks that tended more often than not to overflow and spill onto the floor. Nor had he said anything against the clowns that filled the tops of the shelves and marched across the mantel, replacing the delicate crystal pieces that used to sit on the coffee and end tables in the living room and family room. Pieces she had carefully wrapped and stored in a box so that Cassie could have them one day.

She made a trip to the garage for hammer and nails, several trips to her room for the prints, and within the hour the walls were filled with the rich color of the Alaskan wilderness in moods of each season.

Cold, snowy mountains casting blue shadows, a tiny dog team threading its way at their feet. The silvery flash of a waterfall as it carved a path down the verdant slope of a majestic mountain. Rich reds and gold of autumn, with Mount McKinley hovering in the background, a herd of caribou fat from a summer of grazing dotting the foreground. A wolf and her pups lazily sunning themselves on the tundra.

She moved to the family room and hung one of a red fox caught in the act of emerging from her den, one bright-eyed pup just visible between her dainty forelegs. Then she put up one of an Athabascan woman dressed in traditional garb, dark eyes filled with pride as she cradled her newborn, and another of a woman and small child on the banks of the Yukon River, racks of drying fish in the background.

Each print was full of color and life. Each had its own story to tell. And not a single one matched the furniture.

She then wrapped the displaced prints with a grimace

and placed them in her closet. Just in case Grant disapproved.

The clock in the family room chimed twelve times. Sharon padded around the house in stocking feet, checking all the doors, flicking lights off and turning the heat down. She went to Cassie's room and peeked in. Cassie slept on her side, both hands beneath her cheek, body curved around the circled form of Brittany.

Sharon's heart squeezed with love. She couldn't help but smile as the feeling of well-being washed through her. She returned to her own bed, crawled beneath the covers and flipped the lamp off. Snow whispered against the window. The house settled, groaning a bit beneath the weight of the cold load it held. A hunk of snow broke loose from the metal roof and landed with a thump. She would have to get up early to snow-blow in the morning.

It was a good night to be home.

Home, she thought with a smile. Then she flipped to her stomach, punched the pillow until shapeless and closed her eyes, lulled to sleep by the sound of wind and snow at the window, the creak and groan of the house, comforting in their familiarity.

Hugh called the next evening. Grant answered, stomach tightening instinctively at the sound of Hugh's voice. He could no more stop the reaction than he could the cooling of his tone of voice. Cassie shot a careful look at him before accepting the phone.

He walked over to settle in a chair near the fire. Sharon sat on the hearth, a small frown creasing her brow as she watched Cassie. She turned her gaze to him. "I think you're confusing Cassie," she said in a whisper the little girl could not hear. "You sound so...cold when Hugh calls."

Grant would have liked to argue, but there was nothing

he could say, because he hadn't told her the extent of his problems with Hugh. He should have, but time had gotten away, and Hugh had not contacted him for a few days. He'd hoped the man had finally come to his senses.

"Daddy," Cassie called a few minutes later, "Grandpa wants to talk to you."

Sharon arched a brow. "I'll go tuck Cassie in," she offered. They left the room. Grant took a deep breath, then put the receiver to his ear.

"Dorothy and I would like to come up for a visit," Hugh said.

"Why?" Grant asked flatly.

"Do we need a reason to see our granddaughter?"

He knew they didn't.

"Besides, we want to see for ourselves what this... marriage of yours is like. If it's not in Cassie's best interest—"

"It is." Grant gripped the phone in anger.

"I think that we should be the judge of that," Hugh declared, voice rising to a higher pitch.

There was no point in arguing, so Grant remained silent.

"It will be a short visit," Hugh said in a somewhat calmer voice. "We can stay at a hotel if you prefer."

"You know it would break Cassie's heart if you didn't stay here," Grant said, though each word was so bitter he wanted to spit. They concluded the call. He closed his eyes, letting his head drop back against the love seat.

"Grant?" Sharon said.

Her soft voice almost a caress against his taut nerves. The cushion gave as she sat next to him.

"Hugh and Dorothy are coming to visit for a few days," he said, eyes still closed.

"Soon?"

He could hear the caution in her voice. He nodded, then cracked one eye to look at her.

"I suppose it's inevitable. They're worried about Cassie, and about you." He snorted.

She ignored him. "We really can't fault them for that—now, can we?"

He opened the other eye. "Has anyone ever told you that you're disgustingly fair? Can't you be a little unreasonable for a change? Just once, only for a minute?"

"Oh, I don't know. I've had a few customers at the bank who wouldn't agree." She grinned.

He couldn't help but smile in return, warmth spiraling through him. For just a minute, his gaze held on her lips, and he fought an urge to lean closer. To dip his head as he had the other day and—

"It can't be that bad if they're only staying a few days."

Sharon's words jerked him back to present. The last thing he needed was a repeat of a kiss that should never have happened.

"Sharon, they were...are...very opposed to this marriage. I don't think this is going to be a fun visit. Hugh wants nothing more than to find something wrong, anything, so he can continue the custody battle."

"Oh," she said softly, eyes drifting to her lap for a long minute. Then her chin lifted as she met his gaze. "Well, I guess we'll have to show them that our marriage is happy and loving, and as solid as the mountain out back. And that Cassie could not have a better home, could not be happier."

For just a minute, he wanted to reach over and hug her— something he would have done quite naturally at one time. Before the kiss.

Instead, he said, "Yeah, I guess so. Except it isn't going to be that easy. There is one more problem." She wasn't going to want to hear this any more than he wanted to say the words. "They will be staying here, as in the guest room. Your room."

Her eyes widened. He nodded grimly. She flushed, then said, "Oh," very quietly.

"It gets better," he continued. "We need to move your things into my room, so that it looks like we have…a real marriage." He did not have to say she would be sleeping there.

He was certain she was well aware of the implications.

"Of course," she finally said.

Another long minute of silence stretched between them. Then Sharon lifted her chin and reached to lay a hand on his arm. Slender fingers, unvarnished nails, pale against his dark hair. Warm against his bare flesh. His pulse quickened again. He tried to ignore it, to calm it.

"It's no big deal, Grant. I mean, we have slept together before."

She tried a smile that did not look altogether convincing. Her eyes were wide and dark, as if she needed reassurance.

Reassurance he did not have. "Yeah, but we were kids then. Eight or nine, and in sleeping bags in a tent."

She swallowed hard, her smile dying. "I am sure we can handle it…for just a few days. I mean, what could happen?"

She flushed and looked as if she'd like to take the words back. Grant cursed himself, because he well knew that anything could happen. He was a man, damn it. And she was a far too attractive woman.

"How come you're moving your stuff to Daddy's room?"

Cassie's voice stopped Sharon in midstep the next evening, halfway between her room and Grant's with an armload of dresses. She slowly turned toward the child and took a deep breath.

"Because your grandparents are going to need my room," she answered carefully.

"Oh." Cassie nodded wisely. Sharon continued down the hall. "How come you don't sleep with Daddy, like Mama used to before we moved here?" The little voice followed her.

Sharon didn't face Cassie; instead, she frantically sought a reason she could give the child that would satisfy her. She should have been better prepared, should have known she couldn't put Cassie off until Grant got home, until they could try to explain things together.

"Because…your daddy likes to have lots of room in his bed, and so do I. And he…hogs the pillow, just like Brittany." She mentally cringed, knowing it was a stupid answer, hoping it would satisfy Cassie for the time being. She dreaded the next question, knowing without doubt there would be one. She started to hang her dresses in Grant's closet, next to his shirts.

"Are you gonna have a baby?"

"No," she cried, dropping the dress in her hand and whirling to look at the little girl. "I am not going to have a baby."

Watching Sharon expectantly, with Brittany curled at her side, Cassie perched on the edge of Grant's bed.

A bed that Sharon and Grant would soon be sharing. Warmth flooded Sharon at the thought.

"But that's what happens if you sleep with Daddy. That's what Mama said when he wanted her to come in his room and she wouldn't, and he said he wanted—"

"Cassie, stop. Please." Sharon's heart beat faster than normal. "I don't want to hear about your parents' arguments, okay? That's personal, sort of like a secret. If your daddy wants me to know about that, he'll tell me."

The last thing she needed to hear was that Grant wanted more children, even with a troubled marriage. Which is exactly where that story sounded as though it was heading. A knot tightened in her stomach. Was the bid for a baby a desperate attempt to save the marriage before they learned of the cancer? Or did Grant just want another child regardless? Why would he marry Sharon if he wanted more children? When he said he would never marry again, yet—

Stop! She silently screamed the word. Those were all questions without answers. And she had neither the time nor the emotional resources to deal with them at the moment.

"Cassie, the fact that I don't sleep with your daddy is kind of a secret, also. Our secret—you and me and your daddy. We would like it if you didn't tell anyone else, not even your grandma or grandpa," she said carefully, as if by drawing out the words they would imprint in the little girl's mind.

"Okay." Cassie nodded. Sharon turned to pick up and hang the dress she had dropped.

"Don't you want a baby, Sharon?" Cassie asked softly, hesitantly.

Sharon's heart nearly stopped at the question. "Oh, Cass," she said in a voice choked with anguish. She went to kneel in front of the child, gathered the small hands in her own. She forced a smile. "We don't need to have a baby, to have more children, Cass. We have you, the most wonderful little girl in the world," she said in a husky voice.

Cassie studied her with serious eyes, then her lips curved with a smile. She leaned forward to wrap her arms around Sharon's neck in a tight hug. Sharon hugged back, as tight as she could.

"Sharon is right, Cass."

Sharon's heart slammed in her chest at the sound of Grant's low voice.

"Daddy!" Cassie tore herself from Sharon and ran to Grant. Sharon slowly turned to face him.

"I'm sorry I wasn't here earlier," he said quietly.

She wondered how long he had been standing there, wondered how much he had heard. And wasn't sure she really wanted to know.

Hugh and Dorothy were the first ones off the plane. They hurried across the snowy tarmac into the terminal to gather Cassie in their arms with a cry, with a great deal of hugging and kissing and fussing that grandparents seem to like to do.

Sharon could not help but smile as her heart warmed. "They obviously love her a great deal," she whispered to Grant.

"I never questioned that for a minute," he calmly answered.

Then Hugh separated himself from the flurry of hugs. He was a tall, thin man, with light-blue eyes and closely cut steel-gray hair. "Grant."

He offered his hand along with the quiet greeting. For just a minute, Sharon thought Grant wouldn't accept it, but he did.

Grant gave a brief handshake, uttered a terse, "Hugh." "Sharon."

Hugh turned to her, eyes careful, searching. Dorothy joined them, a petite woman, her head barely reaching Hugh's shoulder, her cropped gray curls a neat cap. Cassie clung to her hand. The older woman's gray eyes brimmed with tears for a few seconds, then she blinked them away and nodded a silent greeting.

Hugh reached to settle his hand along Dorothy's shoulders, a hand that trembled. Compassion rushed through Sharon. It must be awfully hard for them to come to Valdez, to be met by Grant's new wife, the replacement for their daughter. They knew that Grant did not welcome them and probably figured she didn't, either. Hugh and

Dorothy must be wondering where they stood, where they would stand in the end, with this family they no longer belonged to except for Cassie. And now they were preparing to do battle for the grandchild they loved.

Sharon did what seemed the right thing. She stepped forward and offered a hand to Hugh. "Welcome to Valdez." He arched a brow, then slowly took it. Dorothy avoided her eyes, so Sharon refrained from offering her hand in welcome, though she wished it could be otherwise.

"I hope you will enjoy your stay," she said quietly, then stepped back and wrapped her arm through Grant's. His hand settled possessively over hers. She couldn't help but smile up at him. A smile that was easily returned and washed warmth through her.

Hugh cleared his throat. A frown creased his brow. "Well, I suppose we should rent ourselves a car in order to get around while we're here," he said, then turned toward the car rental counter.

"Nonsense," Sharon said firmly. Three pairs of surprised adult eyes swung to her. "You can use mine as long as you don't mind dropping me off at work or picking me up when Grant isn't able to."

"You don't have to do that," Hugh said quietly.

She lifted her chin slightly. "I know that. I would like to."

Hugh and Dorothy hesitated, shot each other guarded glances, then Hugh nodded.

The drive home would have been made in silence if not for Cassie's nearly nonstop chatter. Grant carried luggage into the guest room. Then he joined Sharon in the kitchen, Hugh and Dorothy and Cassie following at his heels.

Grant and Sharon started to prepare dinner, while Cassie flitted back and forth between them and her grandparents, who were seated at the table. The older couple watched like a pair of hawks circling cornered prey.

Grant reached over Sharon to pull a plate down, gently bumping her hip with his to get more room. She arched a brow, then bumped back, grinning while she moved over. She leaned around him to get the seasoning salt, the solid warmth of his body somehow a buffer to the stares she felt trained upon her back.

Cassie dominated the conversation with "Sharon this" or "Brittany that" and "Daddy said." She dragged her grandparents from their vigil to view her framed artwork, then out to the garage to show them her skis. Upon returning to the kitchen, they were given a full accounting of the ski outing.

Hugh and Dorothy hesitated when steaming platters of stir fry and rice were set on the table. Probably wondering if it was poisoned, Sharon couldn't help but thinking. Grant met her gaze and winked as if he read and shared her thought.

The food was plentiful. Conversation was not, except for Cassie's excited jabber.

"Dinner was excellent," Hugh and Dorothy said in near unison. "We'll help clean up."

"Sharon and I can do it," Grant said firmly. "You go on into the family room and I'll start a fire."

Cassie dragged them by the hand as they followed Grant from the kitchen. Sharon felt a blessed quiet, a release from tension.

"Great idea," she told Grant when he returned. "I had no idea how...wearing they were."

"It's not going too bad, is it?" Grant asked.

Sharon's pulse leaped. She ignored it. "I think we're holding our own," she finally said.

He looked as if he was going to say more, then he smiled and started stacking dishes. They worked together, clearing the table, rinsing dishes, loading the dishwasher.

Grant started coffee, and Sharon began loading a plate of cookies.

They turned as one, and bumped into each other. Sharon gasped as cookies started to fall. Grant reached out, grabbing her and the plate, cookies ending up smashed against his chest.

Sharon tried to ignore the strength in his arms and the fact that her heart slammed into her throat so hard that she could barely breathe. She looked down at the cookies, at the chocolate smeared across Grant's shirt. "I don't think we had better serve these," she said.

Grant snorted. She giggled. And they both laughed so hard that Sharon ended up leaning into Grant, unable to stand by herself. The laughter was more a release of tension than anything.

Sharon finally choked back a last chuckle and looked up at Grant. Their eyes caught; his smile died and his eyes darkened. And the tension that suddenly simmered between them had nothing to do with Hugh and Dorothy.

His gaze fastened on her lips. Her throat dried. Then his head slowly lowered—

A throat cleared behind them. They jerked apart.

"We thought we would see if we could help," Dorothy said stiffly, eyes censorious.

Hugh stood behind her, one brow arched. Sharon flushed. She couldn't help herself.

"You can take the coffee mugs. I'll get some more cookies," Grant said easily.

He waited until they left, then he snickered. An honest-to-God snicker that made Sharon laugh in spite of the awkward awareness that still hummed in her veins.

The man who faced her now was the Grant she'd grown up with. Laughter danced in his eyes. A reckless smile transformed his features from handsome to breathtaking.

"Do you feel like we're sixteen again and have just

been caught necking?'' he half whispered, as he dumped the crushed cookies in the trash, then replenished them from the cookie jar, while Sharon poured the coffee into a thermal carafe.

She spoke without thinking, facing him. "At sixteen, you wouldn't have been caught dead necking with me." His smile died and became a frown. She wished she had kept her mouth shut.

"Well, you wouldn't have," she insisted, feeling like a fool for saying anything to begin with, yet also feeling that she needed to defend herself. "You were far too busy with the pretty girls."

She grabbed the coffee carafe and turned to leave, unable to stand another second of his silent scrutiny.

"Sharon."

His quiet voice stopped her midstep. She turned. His dark eyes swept the length of her body, then settled on her face.

"You're a beautiful woman, always were," he said in a husky voice.

Then he stepped around her and walked off. Before her mouth dropped open.

He thought she was beautiful?

No way, she immediately decided. She knew better.

But...Grant wouldn't lie to her. A smile crept across her face. And quite suddenly it didn't matter that she looked the same as yesterday and the day before.

Grant thought she was beautiful, and she couldn't help but feel...well, maybe just a little prettier than she'd thought.

Cassie insisted on being tucked in by her grandparents, then Grant and Sharon. Brittany cried to be let out one last time just as Grant got Cassie settled.

"I'll do it," Sharon offered, then took the pup down

the hall. Cassie was half-asleep when she returned, with Grant nowhere to be seen. Sharon refused to dwell on the fact that he probably waited in his bedroom. Their bedroom.

You're a beautiful woman...

His words returned, unwanted, unbidden. As was the shiver of awareness that accompanied them.

Brittany bounded onto the bed and curled up next to the little girl.

"I love you, Sharon," Cassie whispered, then rolled over and buried her face in the pup.

"I love you, too," Sharon murmured past the sudden lump in her throat. She turned and was startled to see Dorothy standing in the doorway, silently watching.

"I just wanted to check on her one last time," the older woman said, chin lifting slightly, as if in defense of her actions.

"Of course," Sharon said quietly, then stepped around her to leave the room. She wished with each step she took down the hall, that she was not so aware of Grant as a man, that he did not have the power with a few simple words, with a single glance, to make her feel more a woman than ever before. She knew too well that she had needs that would not be met, because their relationship could never be more than just friends.

Grant was sitting on the bed, a bed that seemed to have shrunk in size since yesterday. She took a deep breath and walked over to sit next to him. Close, but not too close.

"Well, I think we did all right tonight." She met Grant's gaze and could not look away. The darkness in his eyes seemed to pull at her, to hold her transfixed. She became even more aware that the bed they sat on would be where she—*they* would be sleeping for the next few nights.

She jerked her gaze away, pulse racing. She stood, unable to remain at his side any longer, then went over to the dresser to dig out a fresh pair of pajamas.

"Sharon."

She almost cried out at Grant's husky voice, and slowly turned to face him. He held out a large shopping bag.

"I got you something on the way home from work." He had trouble meeting her eyes.

She laid her pajamas on the dresser and took the bag, surprised, then a little wary because of his obvious discomfort. She reached in and pulled out a robe. "Oh" was all she could say as she held it out: thick, nubby material, with a large plastic zipper that ran up the front, neck to toe. Multicolored, with huge splashes of brilliant pink, purple and red. She swallowed hard and carefully reached into the bag once more. A flannel nightgown, red-and-white candy striped, red heart-shaped buttons the size of quarters, starting at the chest up to the neck. A broad ruffle of lace at the neck and at the wrists.

She stared at it for one long minute, then slowly closed her mouth, wondering how long it had been hanging open. "It's...ah—"

"All they had," Grant said grimly.

She met his gaze, and wondered how long she had to wear the robe and nightgown before giving them to the secondhand store.

He studied her quietly, frowning. "They were on sale," he added.

You paid money for these, she wanted to cry. Instead, she said, "They are...unique." She didn't want to offend him, yet she was horrified he would think she would like this...this—

"'Horrible' might be more accurate." One corner of his mouth twitched at the statement.

"Well..." She frantically searched for words. "'Hideous' is actually what I had in mind,'' she finally said, honesty winning out as it always did.

He laughed, a burst of real humor that nearly left her gaping. His eyes were suddenly dancing, his features transformed to sheer beauty that had her heart catching. Answering laughter bubbled from within her, joining his to fill the room. Full-bodied, unrestrained laughter that had as much to do with release of tension as it did the garments she held in her hands.

"Why?" She gasped and threw the nightgown at him. It caught on his head, then slid to drape around his shoulders for a few seconds before falling to the bed. "What did I do to deserve this?"

He merely shook his head, held his sides and barked more laughter. Sharon stumbled to the bed, where she dropped by his side, then fell back, holding her stomach. "Stop," she gasped. "Please."

"I'm trying." He choked the words out.

The bed shook with their laughter. She rolled to her side and buried her face in the robe. Finally, Grant drew a deep breath and stopped laughing. Sharon held her breath, gasped and managed to stop her laughter.

Grant looked at her, eyes filled with humor, face creased with a smile. Then his smile faded, his eyes darkened.

"You have to wear this while we're sleeping together," he said. A muscle in his jaw tightened.

"But I have pajamas—"

He reached to still her with a touch of a finger to her lips. Her words died as her pulse leaped.

"Sharon, your pajamas are far too revealing," he said quietly.

Her mouth dropped open. She almost argued that they were just like shorts and a tank top. Then she snapped her jaw shut as the implication of what Grant had said sank in.

Her throat dried and she suddenly became aware that she was lying on his bed, a bed they were getting ready to share. Heat from his thigh penetrated hers, and fear and longing swept her. Fear that had her barely resisting the urge to jump up and run from the room. And longing that had her aching to be held by Grant—man to woman—just once.

She could not do this, she silently screamed.

She had to, she grimly told herself.

She could well imagine Hugh's and Dorothy's reaction as she ran shrieking past their bedroom. Neither she nor Grant could elect to sleep on the couch if they wanted the marriage to look real and happy.

"Well...we had better get some sleep," Grant said, sounding as if he was suggesting an execution. "Are you going to be okay with...this?"

Did they have a choice? Sharon swallowed the words because they would accomplish nothing, then nodded. "We'll just pretend we're in the tent in our sleeping bags," she said in a half whisper, then cleared her throat.

"Yeah, well, at least we don't have to worry about my brothers sneaking out in the middle of the night and shaking the tent, growling like bears. You damned near broke my eardrums when you screamed." His eyes warmed with the memory.

Sharon couldn't help but laugh. A small, shaky laugh that would have made her feel better if not for the fact that he was right. No one was going to bother them here. It was going to be just the two of them. All night long.

"You can have the bathroom first," he said quietly.

She slid from the bed and hurried into the adjoining bathroom. The nightgown was as horrible on as off. One look at her and Grant was likely to be the one to run shrieking from the room. For her to be unalluring was what they wanted, she reminded herself, then pulled the robe on and nearly gasped when she gazed in the mirror.

Grant looked up when she walked into the room.

"If you laugh, you're dead," she said grimly.

He paused. "I'd say we needn't worry about any... anything now," he said carefully.

She marched to the bed, shed the robe and slipped beneath the covers with as much dignity as she could. She silently dared Grant—one snort, one cackle of laughter and *he* would be wearing the nightgown.

Grant went into the bathroom. A few minutes later he returned, the door closing behind him with a click. Sharon's breath caught. She refused to watch as Grant settled on the bed, the scent of soap filling the air. Her heart dipped with the mattress, then slammed into an uneven gallop when he flipped off the lamp, flooding the room in darkness and unwanted intimacy.

The blankets lifted, then fell as he slid beneath them. They both lay on their sides, back to back, each poised on their respective edges of the mattress, uncomfortably aware of each other.

It should have been funny. They should have been able to laugh the situation off, turn it into a joke. But somehow the humor just wasn't there. And it was nothing—no big deal—just like sleeping in the tent when they were kids.

Chapter Eight

Every time Grant started to drift off to sleep, he would relax and shift, move an arm or a leg and brush up against Sharon. Then he would jerk awake as if poked by an electric cattle prod. Eyes wide. Every cell in his body on full alert. Totally aware that a woman lay sleeping next to him.

A very desirable woman.

Sharon, he reminded himself. She apparently did not share his awareness, his difficulty in sleeping. Her breathing was soft, even, and drew images to mind that he had no business entertaining.

He swallowed a groan and forced the images away, trying to remember Sharon at eight, as a skinny thing with gangly legs and arms, a face full of freckles that had somehow thinned with time, a head of wild curly hair that he used to tease her endlessly about.

Instead, he remembered a pair of soft brown eyes washing warmth over him, a cap of silken russet curls he longed to bury his face in and a smile that could melt icebergs. All woman, and far too inviting.

All he had to do was roll over and reach out, and she would be in his arms.

He rolled onto his stomach to bury his face in the pillow. The scent of her perfume seemed to surround him. Even though he hugged the edge of the bed, could not get any farther away without landing on his butt on the floor, heat seemed to permeate the small space between them, to reach out with a silent invitation that promised relief of one kind and torture of another.

He fought the invitation and dozed in fits and starts until four-thirty in the morning. Then he finally gave up, tip-toeing to his dresser for clothes, into the bathroom for a quick shower and to dress. Then he crept like a silent ghost through the house to the kitchen.

He started the coffeemaker and stood next to the window, staring out at the darkness punctuated by stabs of light from the streetlights. A light flickered on here, one over there, in the houses below as Valdez slowly awoke. Snow began to trickle from the sky. When the coffee was ready, he flipped the deck light on, settled in a chair with a steaming mug and watched as the snow thickened. Soon it was coming down in a heavy sheet.

"Still an early riser, I see."

Hugh's quiet voice startled him. Grant slowly turned to face the man.

"Where's Sharon?"

"Still in bed," Grant answered.

"I see," Hugh said dryly.

And Grant wondered if he did.

"I know it's not easy for you to have us stay here," Hugh said, "but we...do appreciate it."

"I did it for Cassie," Grant answered.

Hugh opened his mouth as if to speak, then closed it. He cleared his throat, turned toward the coffeemaker. "Can I join you for a cup of coffee?"

Though Grant and Hugh had a long tradition of early-morning coffee when visiting each other, Grant wasn't sure he could sit across from Hugh and act as if the battle lines hadn't been drawn, with both of them clearly on opposite sides and Hugh the instigator.

"Help yourself. I need to get to work," he said quietly.

He rose and walked from the room before he changed his mind. Before he let himself wonder why Hugh would expect an early-morning truce when he was the initiator of the war. Before he let himself care.

Sharon rolled over onto her stomach, wrapping her arms around the pillow and burying her face in it. A pillow that smelled like Grant. She inhaled deeply until she realized what she was doing. Then she shot up out of bed, wide-awake, heart suddenly pounding harder. Heat burned her cheeks. Grant was nowhere in sight, and his pajamas lay in a heap on the floor by the dresser. She glanced at the clock on the nightstand and muttered an oath. She had slept later than intended.

She grabbed clothes out of the closet and dresser, then hurried into the bathroom for a quick shower and to dress. The house was oddly quiet—no sign of Cassie or Brittany, Hugh or Dorothy. Or Grant.

Dorothy was in the kitchen, seated at the table, sipping a mug of coffee. "Cassie and Hugh went for a walk with Brittany. Grant left for work quite early. I hope you don't mind that I helped myself to coffee," she said stiffly. Her eyes were cold and careful, anything but welcoming.

Sizing up your adversary? Sharon wanted to ask. Instead, she said, "Of course not. We want you to make yourselves at home," and forced a smile. "Would you like some breakfast?"

The older woman shook her head. Sharon poured a mug

of coffee and a bowl of cereal, added milk, then walked to the table to sit opposite Dorothy.

Dorothy broke the silence. "It was good of you and Grant to let us stay." Lips pinched together in a thin line, she looked as if the words had a bad taste.

Sharon captured the other woman's gaze. "You will always be welcome here because you're family."

Dorothy's eyes widened a bit. She started to say something, then stopped, lowered her gaze, stared at her mug and said, "Thank you," in a slightly husky voice. She cleared her throat and raised her gaze.

Sharon met her gaze with a steady one of her own. "I don't agree with what you and Hugh are doing, but I think it's more important to put aside our differences while you're here. For Cassie's sake. Grant and I want nothing more than her happiness."

Sharon started eating when Dorothy didn't answer. She was nearly finished with the cereal, when Dorothy spoke. "Hugh mentioned that your families approved of this... marriage." The woman sounded unbelieving.

"Very much. My parents love Grant."

"Where are your parents? Your family?"

"I'm an only child, and my parents are living in Arizona now. After nearly forty years of long Alaskan winters, my mother swore she wanted nothing but heat. Lots of hot, sunny days." She smiled. "She still refuses to come back, even for a visit."

"Catherine didn't like Alaska. She was miserable here. I suppose it didn't help that divorce was imminent," Dorothy said quietly.

Sharon remained silent, unaware what Catherine's feelings had been about Alaska, shocked to learn that Grant's marriage had been on the verge of divorce. She'd known it was troubled, but not the extent.

"You must like it."

Dorothy's words jerked her back to present. "I suppose it's different for me, since I grew up here. It's home. Sure, the winters are long and dark, so by spring you're gnashing your teeth. But on a clear, sunny day, winter or summer alike, you simply won't find a place more beautiful than Valdez. I love the wilderness, the water and mountains. Seeing eagles soar overhead and never knowing when I might spot a black bear when hiking up Mineral Creek. I even like snow, which is good, because we get a bunch of it.

"The small-town atmosphere. The people. And if you've ever seen the northern lights dancing above the mountain ridges..." She shook her head. "I just can't imagine living anywhere else," she finished quietly.

Dorothy studied her over the rim of her mug. "We were naturally quite surprised when Grant decided to get married so quickly. Are you pregnant?"

Sharon sputtered, nearly choking on her coffee, and set the mug firmly on the table. She stared at the older woman, battling the urge to tell her to mind her own business. She finally shook her head. "No, I am not."

"I see. We...well, we couldn't help but be curious. The swiftness of your marriage, the fact that it is...so soon after Catherine..." Her words died. She took a quick swallow of her coffee, hands trembling slightly. "Hugh and I...we were afraid maybe we forced Grant into marriage by our actions. I told him, of course, that Grant isn't the type to be forced into anything he doesn't want." She paused.

Sharon, wondering if she dared try more coffee, lifted the cup.

"Are you planning a family?"

Sharon set the cup down with a sigh. "No," she said quietly, wishing with all her heart she could get angry with the woman and knowing that she wouldn't. Better that the questions be asked and gotten out of the way.

"I love Cassie," she continued. "I have always loved children, but Grant and I have decided not to have more children." She forgave herself the white lie, since it was only half a lie. Since she and Grant never planned to be intimate, that certainly ruled out the possibility of more family. And Dorothy did not need to know that Sharon could not have children.

Grant found Sharon in the bedroom that evening. "I'm sorry I wasn't here earlier."

She shrugged, and began to hang her business suit in the closet. "I just got home myself. Dorothy and Hugh have offered to treat us to dinner."

She turned to face him, paused as if she wanted to say more, then started for the door, stopped and turned back. She walked to stand in front of him. Her gaze was troubled when it met his and he couldn't help but stiffen just a bit at the serious look in her eyes.

"Why didn't you tell me that you and Catherine were ready to divorce?"

Her question hit him square in the stomach like a solid blow that had him catching his breath.

"It doesn't seem the sort of thing I should hear second-hand."

"You knew we were having problems."

"Yes, but problems do not necessarily mean divorce."

He took a deep breath. "What is it exactly that you wanted to know?" he asked quietly. They were but inches apart, the scent of her perfume wafting to him. "The fact that I made my wife miserable? That no matter how hard I tried, I couldn't make Catherine happy?"

Cold shame trembled through him. He looked away, not able to stand seeing the disappointment certain to be reflected in Sharon's eyes.

She reached to lay a hand on his shoulder. A steady

touch of comfort. "I don't know what happened in your marriage, Grant, but I do know that you are not responsible for other people's happiness. You can add or detract from it, but in the end, only they can be responsible. Except, of course, for very small children, and Catherine was no child."

"You don't know what you're talking about."

"Then maybe you should explain," she said.

Her hand remained. He could have shrugged it off, walked away. He didn't. She had a right to know the whole truth.

"Catherine hated Alaska," he said reluctantly. "She hated Alaska, and when I refused to move, she hated me." The words started hard and slow, then sped up. "She was getting ready to divorce me, when she found out she was sick. And she made it clear that if it wasn't for the misery I'd caused her all those years, she would have had a life worth living. She told me I caused her cancer."

Sharon gasped.

He continued in a low tone. "Even though I know I didn't, sometimes I can't help but wonder if her unhappiness did contribute to the illness."

He drew a shaky breath. His voice grew husky. "Nothing I did was right. Good enough. Though, God knows, I tried everything." His hands clenched into fists. A shudder ran through his body, though he tried to suppress it. "Any love we had died long before Catherine did. Long before," he finished hoarsely.

He closed his eyes and wished he had kept his mouth shut. A chill raced through him and his stomach twisted painfully. He felt weak, stripped naked and exposed, unable to stop the emotion that still trembled through him like leaves on the wind, although he did not move a muscle.

"She was wrong," Sharon said quietly in a shaky voice

that grew stronger as she continued. "Maybe she didn't like Alaska, but she made the decision to marry you knowing you were going to live here. Her choice, Grant. As for staying, she made that choice, too. If she hated it...or you so much, she could have left years ago. And I cannot believe that anyone...anyone would accuse another person of causing an illness that is so little understood. I cannot believe—" Her voice broke. She drew a deep breath. "I'm sorry that your marriage turned bad," she said more calmly.

Her words chipped away at the hardened layers of guilt and shame, of self-condemnation. She went on. "But I know, as clearly as I know night from day, that it was not your fault. It takes two to make a marriage. And no one can *make* someone happy. That lies within each and every person, and they alone are responsible for their own happiness."

He moved so that they were facing once more, forced himself to meet her eyes. "You might as well hear the rest," he said quietly.

She nodded, gaze steady.

"Hugh and Dorothy blamed me, also." He shook his head, suddenly tired. "They didn't come right out and say it, but I saw it in their eyes, their actions."

He swallowed hard. "They pushed me away when I needed their support. I suppose it was selfish on my part, maybe demanding something I didn't have a right to, but I needed their help, damn it. They blamed me, instead, turned a cold shoulder. I cared for those two as if they were family." His voice became raspy. He cleared his throat.

"So, right or wrong—" he drew a deep breath "—maybe you can see why I find it a little hard to forgive them for what they're doing now. To welcome them into my home with open arms."

Sharon stepped forward, wrapped her arms around him in a hug, laying her head against his shoulder. "I'm so sorry," she whispered roughly, then cleared her throat. "Hugh and Dorothy were wrong, so very wrong."

Her words flowed over him, through him, a soothing balm to raw nerves. He couldn't help but pull her to him a little closer. To hold her tightly in his arms, needing her touch.

She eased back a bit to raise up on tiptoe to brush a kiss against his cheek. It grazed the corner of his mouth. A brush of lips he turned to meet as naturally as if they had planned it.

She hesitated, then melted against him, lips eager and searching as they met his. He wanted to deepen the kiss. Wanted to pull her over to the bed, forget Hugh and Dorothy and Cassie, forget dinner. To lay Sharon down on the bed, peel her clothes off and—

She moaned. They both jerked apart as if just realizing what they were doing.

"I'm sorry," he said hoarsely.

She pressed her fingers to his lips briefly to silence him. Her eyes were wide, dark; her cheeks flushed. He fought the urge to pull her into his arms again and damned himself the need.

"Don't be sorry," Sharon finally managed in a half whisper. "It isn't your fault. There's nothing to blame."

She trembled inside as she stared at Grant. Her own words echoed in her mind. She could still feel the warmth, the hard strength of his lips, and her heart leaped at the memory, at the fact that she wanted nothing more than to step forward, to wrap her arms around his neck and be lost to another kiss.

Because she loved him.

Shocked, she could only stare at him, trace his lean jaw,

the line of his lips, with her eyes. And ache for more. Much more. And wonder if she had lost her mind.

"I'd better clean up," he finally said, then turned and strode into the bathroom.

The door closed behind him, but the image of long, well-muscled legs clad in jeans, of broad shoulders and dark, glittering eyes, remained.

She sank to the bed. She couldn't love Grant. It wasn't part of the plan. Wasn't something he would want or welcome. She *had* lost her mind, along with every lick of sense she'd ever had.

Yet even as she tried to deny it, the truth grew stronger and more shatteringly clear.

She loved Grant as she had no other man. A love born in childhood, put aside for lack of hope and resurfacing now with a strength that frightened her.

When could this have happened without her realizing it? Her mind traveled back in time. There was no single event, no great moment of truth until now. Although she had always admitted her love for Grant as a friend, had it been more all along? Would she have proposed this marriage if it hadn't been?

Probably not, she realized with cold dread. And Grant would have never agreed if he had known. Just because she'd been deluding herself all these years didn't change the fact that Grant had never been interested in her. Had never wanted her love, and was not likely to welcome it any more now.

What had she gotten herself into? A wave of nausea rolled through her. She closed her eyes, swallowed hard and took several deep, steadying breaths.

What she had gotten herself into was being a mother to Cassie, she told herself firmly, something she would never regret. And she was helping a friend in dire need. Just because she happened to love Grant didn't change a thing.

If only she were whole, she would—

Do nothing, she told herself with a mental shake. Which was exactly what she was going to do now. Grant would never know her true feelings.

Grant worked late the next night, through dinner and well past Cassie's bedtime. He had not wanted to, but had to put in the long hours to prepare a presentation to the owner companies the following morning.

The garage lights beckoned as he pulled into the driveway, but silence greeted him as he walked into the darkened house. Although exhausted by hours of meetings, he was too wound up to sleep. Massaging the back of his neck, he toed off his shoes and padded on stocking feet to the kitchen, heading for the fridge without turning on the light.

"There's leftover Chinese food," Hugh said.

Grant spun around at the unexpected sound of a voice, his heart in his throat.

"I'm sorry if I startled you," Hugh added. He sat at the table, elbows on the surface, chin resting on his hands. A mellow glow from the deck light washed across him.

He looked...older. Grant couldn't stop the pang at the thought.

"There's something so very peaceful about watching it snow," Hugh said. He started to say more, then stopped. Their gazes caught and held. "You and Sharon seem to get along well," Hugh said softly.

Grant tensed, surprised.

Hugh shrugged with a wry grin that quickly faded. "I suppose we hoped to find...well, I'm not sure...that maybe you didn't get along. That maybe the marriage was nothing but a sham." He shook his head. "It's obvious that you love each other a great deal. I am sorry we so misjudged you."

How in the hell Hugh had gotten the idea that he and Sharon were in love was beyond Grant. He had no clue what to say. He couldn't very well argue that Hugh was wrong, that Sharon and he were nothing more than friends.

"I've been doing a lot of thinking since we've been here," Hugh continued. "And talking with Dorothy." He paused, then cleared his throat. "It's obvious that Cassie loves Sharon and that...she is happy." He lowered his voice. "It isn't easy to see that life goes on without our Catherine, but we have had to face some very hard truths."

His face suddenly looked haggard. Grant almost asked him to stop.

"We owe you an apology for many things, Grant. Not the least of...how we acted when Catherine was ill." His voice died to a whisper.

Grant wanted to ask, why? Why had they backed away when Catherine was ill? Why had they turned a cold shoulder when he had needed them the most? Challenged him for custody of his own daughter? And how could they expect forgiveness with a simple apology? Only words. Words could not erase the pain he still felt at the memory.

And yet...he turned around and almost stepped forward. He opened his mouth to speak, then closed it. A shudder ran through him. He could not afford to resurrect the pain they had caused. "Forget it," he said gruffly, the closest to forgiveness that he could manage at the moment. Hugh waited, silent. Then Grant walked from the room.

Sharon was in bed reading, lamplight puddling around her. Grant hesitated at the door, then slowly closed it behind him.

"Did you see Hugh? He was going to wait up for you." She set the book aside.

He nodded, unable to speak.

"Did you talk?" she asked softly.

"Sort of, I mean, not really," he finally managed.

She wavered, then spoke again. "I think you should, Grant. I know it's hard, but...well, we talked a little tonight. Hugh and Dorothy and I. I think...I know they're hurting inside."

"Good," Grant said, though he didn't mean it. "What do you think it does to me?" He tried to find his old anger, the pain. He found a weary cynicism, instead. A fear that, maybe, he couldn't forgive anymore. That he didn't have it in him.

The thought sickened him. He sank to the foot of the bed and dropped his head into his hands. "I don't know," he half whispered. "I just don't know."

He wasn't sure who he was talking to, or even what he meant. Long-buried emotion welled up from within. He couldn't push it away and couldn't control it any longer.

"Go talk with him," Sharon said quietly. She moved to sit behind him, hands rubbing his shoulders in strong, comforting strokes. He wanted to sink back into her softness, to turn and gather her in his arms and forget that anyone else existed for the moment. It wasn't a physical need as much as a mental need for comfort.

"I'm not sure I can forgive him," he said reluctantly.

Her hands didn't miss a stroke. "You can."

He half smiled at the certainty in her voice. He might have doubts, but Sharon apparently didn't.

"I could come with you," she offered.

"No." He shook his head. "This is something I need to do alone."

Yet the fact that she had wanted to, that she was there, encouraging with words as well as touch, gave him strength. Her gentle reassurance convinced him.

He reached up and captured her hands in his, squeezed them briefly, then stood and walked from the room, back down the darkened hall. His throat dried. His hands curled into fists at his side, and every muscle in his body tensed like a taut barbed-wire fence.

For a minute, he thought the kitchen was empty. Then he heard a harsh sob and froze. Hugh stood in the shadows by the window, forehead leaning into the pane, shoulders shaking.

Pain shot through Grant as Hugh sobbed again. Pain that only added to his sadness and didn't accomplish one damned thing. "No." The single word tore from the depths of his soul. He strode forward and grasped Hugh's shoulder. Hugh stiffened, tried to pull away, but Grant refused to let him.

And then suddenly they were in each other's arms. Clinging to each other as men rarely do, in the safety of darkness. Unexpected compassion swept Grant at the thinness of the man he held. At the fragile vulnerability he was suddenly too aware of. Hugh's choked sobs, his harsh breathing, tore at Grant unrelentingly, like a giant fist that wasn't satisfied, until tears ran down his own cheeks. Until their pain joined and he wasn't sure who was comforting whom.

Finally, they stopped. Hugh shuddered. "We sound like a couple of old women, don't we?"

Grant drew a deep breath, fought a wave of embarrassment and suppressed an unexpected chuckle.

"Well—" Hugh pulled away, but not too far. "At least there aren't any witnesses."

Grant did chuckle then. A brief rumble of humor, fueled as much by relief as anything. Hugh chuckled, too. Then he stilled, reached a hand to lay on Grant's shoulder and met his gaze. "I would like to try to explain," he said quietly.

The simple words, the naked plea in Hugh's eyes, stripped Grant of his last defense. This was a man he had loved once, still loved, and he could no longer deny it. He nodded, then they sat on the kitchen chairs, confession easier given when shrouded in heavy dusk and shadow.

Words rolled from Hugh as water from a floodgate. Of how he and Dorothy had been so angered and pained by Catherine's illness they had sought to blame someone. Anyone. And Grant was a convenient target. They had pushed away his need. Pushed away logic. And replaced it with anger and fear and grief.

"You aren't the only one we did it to. Ask all our family and friends. And when Catherine was…gone, we sort of went crazy. Terrified that we had lost you. Certain that we would lose Cassie and somehow, in our convoluted thinking, managing to convince ourselves that you shouldn't have her." He sighed. "I guess maybe we were trying to replace what couldn't be. Catherine."

He paused. "When you married Sharon, well…that was the last straw. Our fears of losing Cassie were suddenly real. I mean, Sharon has her own family, and you, yours. You didn't need us anymore."

Grant started to protest. Hugh held up his hand to silence him. "We came here ready to fight for Cassie, and instead realized that she's happy."

"She'll never forget Catherine. We won't let her," Grant softly promised.

Hugh nodded, silent for a minute, then cleared his throat. "I know things will never be the same…but I hope you can find it in your heart to forgive us one day."

Forgiveness. An ability Grant didn't believe he possessed anymore. It would be safer, easier, to take a step back and gain some distance. Then he remembered Sharon's quiet conviction that he could and would do the right thing. A sense of peace, a sense of strength, washed through him.

"Seems we're already halfway there," he said.

* * *

Sharon was sleeping by the time Grant returned to the room. He found his pajamas, slipped into them, then tiptoed to her side of the bed. He studied her for one long minute. Face framed by a halo of curls. One hand curled next to her cheek as she slept on her side.

He reached to brush a knuckle against her cheek, and ached to wake her and talk. Just talk, he told himself. Friend to friend, because that was what she was. Without her, he would not have returned to talk with Hugh. And now he felt a tremendous weight had been lifted from his shoulders. He traced her jaw, unable to resist touching her once more. Then he picked up the book she had been reading, which lay on the floor, and snapped off the lamp.

He slid into his side of the bed, closed his eyes. Her gentle breathing filled the air. Her warmth seemed to reach out to him. She rolled to her back with a soft snore, hand nesting at her waist, face illuminated by the glow of the clock radio.

Grant stared at her hand for several seconds, then reached to trace the back of it from the wrist down, to cup it, her fingers curling to fit in the palm of his hand as if they belonged there. He didn't understand this compelling need to touch her but couldn't resist it, either, if only for a minute.

It didn't frighten him, perhaps because he was too damned tired to expend the energy. He closed his eyes and drifted off to sleep, Sharon's hand curled within his own.

Hugh and Dorothy left two days later. "You take care of that girl. She loves you very much," Hugh instructed Grant as they loaded luggage.

"I always take care of Cassie," Grant reminded him.

"I was talking about Sharon."

Dorothy pulled him to one side at the airport. "I know it's none of my business, but I wish you and Sharon would reconsider your decision not to have children. You're both wonderful parents."

Grant barely stopped his mouth from dropping open. Dorothy patted him on the arm.

"Think about it," she said.

Cassie cried. Hugh and Dorothy and Sharon hugged and kissed.

Then Hugh stepped over to Grant. "Well..." He held out a hand.

Grant looked down at it and up at the man. Then he stepped forward to give Hugh a long, hard hug.

"You come and see us, you hear." Hugh's eyes glistened when he stepped back. Grant nodded, unable to speak past the lump in his throat. He lifted a crying Cassie in his arms. Sharon stood at his side. And they watched as the elderly couple slowly made their way out to the plane.

Although Sharon slept in her own room that night, her presence seemed to fill Grant's room. He expected to fall asleep immediately. Yet when he lay on his back and stared at the ceiling, images of Sharon crept into his mind. Halo of curls spilling on the pillow, framing her face. Thick lashes kissing creamy cheeks. Desire whispered to life, the last thing he wanted or needed. He rolled over and buried his face in the pillow with a groan. A pillow her scent clung to.

He pushed it off the bed, fisted his hands at his side and willed himself to sleep—an action about as effective as cleaning snow from the driveway with a tablespoon.

When he found himself savoring the memory of their kiss, a memory he had thrust from his mind with the greatest of efforts until now, he muttered an oath. He finally slept, a restless sleep interspersed with wisps of dreams about Sharon. Dreams that expressed in sleep thoughts he would never allow while awake. He woke up tired and angry at himself for having so little control over his mind.

A pair of panty hose hung from the shower nozzle. He stared at them one long minute, then removed them, handling them as carefully as if they were a bomb ready to explode. He returned to take a shower. As water cascaded over his body, he imagined Sharon's hands doing the same. He swore under his breath when he realized what he was doing. He reached for the shampoo and found himself massaging his scalp with lemon-scented suds.

It was hopeless, he decided with a sigh. This desire that sang through his veins was stronger than he was. Somehow he was going to have to conquer it and he hadn't the slightest idea how.

Maybe it would run its course and die of its own volition. Or maybe he should suggest to Sharon that they include a physical aspect to their marriage.

Yeah, right. And maybe she would tell him exactly where to go.

And maybe not.

The thought stilled his hands. Then he resumed massaging shampoo into his scalp. While he had been the one to initiate the kiss, she'd certainly been willing.

It wasn't as if they had to be in love to satisfy mutual desires. And Sharon was a healthy, attractive woman. Certainly she must have needs that mirrored his own.

He snorted and stepped beneath the spray of water. The suds washed away, but his thoughts didn't.

Chapter Nine

Cassie was at a slumber party. Sharon took it as a good sign the little girl was secure enough to want to spend the night away from home. Yet…the silence of the house pressed around her, almost suffocating.

Brittany was busy chewing a leather bone. Grant should be home any minute. And Sharon was filled with a restless energy. She went into the kitchen, put rice on to cook, pulled chicken and vegetables from the fridge. She was cutting and chopping when Grant walked in.

"I was going to suggest we eat out," he said. He brushed past her to get in the fridge, the scent of cold air, a hint of after-shave following.

She shrugged casually, though every nerve in her body went on full alert like finely tuned radar, brought alive by Grant. By the fact that he stood but inches away. Shirt sleeves rolled to his elbow. Muscle taut in his forearm.

He snapped the tab on a can of soda. She jumped. He tilted the can back for a long swallow and Sharon couldn't draw her gaze away from his neck, to the muscle that worked there. He lowered the can; she whirled to face the counter, pulse pounding.

If this was what being in love with Grant was going to do to her, she wanted no part of it.

"Dinner will be ready in a few minutes," she said, grateful that the words were steady, though her hands trembled as she chopped mushrooms.

"I'll set the table."

He moved closer and reached up past her for the plates. Her heart skipped and she missed the mushroom she was chopping, neatly slicing the end of her finger, instead.

She cried out and dropped the knife. Grant grabbed for a dish towel and wrapped her finger in it. "What the hell are you trying to do?" he snapped, dragging her to the sink to run water over the cut.

"Adding extra protein?" she offered weakly. His touch was causing more havoc than the cut. "I'm fine, Grant." She started to pull her hand away. He refused to relinquish it, instead reaching for a first-aid kit from under the sink. A minute later he had wrapped a bandage around the finger.

"There."

He looked up; their gazes caught and locked. They were but inches apart. His breath caressed her cheek. He still held her hand, eyes widening, then darkening. Sharon's legs turned to jelly. She could not have moved even if she had wanted to.

Just this once, she told herself, as Grant stepped closer, lowered his head and captured her lips with his. A tentative kiss at first that quickly deepened. Became demanding, devouring. She didn't give an inch, met his need, his demand, with one of her own.

He dragged her nearer, hands cupping her hips. She pressed against him, arms winding around his neck in a fierce grip. She moaned; he swallowed it. His fingers dug into her hips, bespeaking an urgency that also roared in her veins. He finally groaned, then pulled his head away, buried his face in her neck. His breathing was harsh, as ragged as her own. Part of her wanted to cry out in protest and continue the embrace. The other part thanked God for small moments of sanity.

"We can't do this," Grant said hoarsely.

"I know," she whispered, heart still pounding madly. But she wanted to. Oh, how she wanted to.

"It wasn't…isn't part of the bargain." He pulled back to capture her gaze. "Unless you want to change it."

Her heart nearly stopped.

His eyes never left her face.

"I'm not suggesting that we take it beyond the physical. I mean…well, we like each other, and we're both obviously…attracted to each other. We both have needs." His voice grew husky.

She turned away before she threw herself back into his arms. Thought and emotion whirled through her mind; she couldn't think clearly. Could only feel the want, the horrible overwhelming ache she had to say yes.

He stepped closer again, the heat of his body penetrating her clothing, calling to her body, drawing a response she hadn't the strength to deny.

"Lord knows, I have fought it, Sharon. But I want you."

She choked back a sob. His hands settled on her shoulders. He dropped a kiss on her neck.

She should walk away from his touch.

She leaned into him, instead.

"I want you, Sharon. And I think you want me."

Just this once, she thought. God forgive her, she wanted to make love to Grant.

"We could have children. You've always wanted a large family. A little girl who looks just like you and—"

She whirled to face him, horror rushing through her. She fought the urge to be sick. He wanted children.

"I thought you didn't want more children," she cried. "You said you didn't. That you didn't even want to marry. You don't love me."

He frowned, then spoke. "I did. Didn't, I mean. But...well...I wouldn't mind children all that much."

All Sharon could do was back away, one slow step at a time. "No." she shook her head. "No. This is not a good idea."

Grant closed his eyes briefly, took a deep breath, nostrils flaring. "Okay," he finally said, then attempted a half smile that failed. He took another deep breath, then shoved his hands into his pockets. "I'm sorry."

It was all she could do not to step forward and wrap her arms around him. And give him what they both wanted, if only for the night.

"Maybe we should eat out after all."

His husky voice sent shivers along her spine and urged her to step forward once again.

If she did, it wouldn't stop there.

She gathered her resolve, then turned and started putting food away. Her hands trembled so badly she could hardly pick up the vegetables. If only—

She squashed the thought immediately. "If only" didn't count.

Because Grant wanted children, and she couldn't give them to him.

If Grant had hoped to kill his desire by going to a restaurant, he failed. Though he had eaten there countless times before, the darkened interior of the steak house suddenly seemed intimate. The dusky light caressed Sharon's features, added intriguing shadows he wanted to explore.

The drink he ordered did little to erase her taste, or the

memory of her touch, the feel of her hands at the back of his neck. Her breasts crushed against his chest, her heart joining his in a pounding dance of rising passion.

He stifled a groan. And wondered how he had managed to sleep in the same bed with her and not reach over and take advantage.

Because, he reminded himself, that is exactly what he would have been doing. Taking advantage. It didn't matter that Sharon had reciprocated the kiss while in his arms. What mattered was that they stuck to what they had agreed to, and not complicate matters with a short-lived affair that would cause more problems than it solved.

An affair she had made obvious she did not want, regardless of her physical needs. He was not likely to forget her look of horror when he'd suggested that they could have children. He supposed he could have told her how much he cared for her, if that would have made a difference.

His stomach knotted at the thought. He was treading on dangerous ground now. If he couldn't give her his heart, why lead her to believe any different? He would endure cold showers every night for the rest of his life before he took her to his bed unwillingly.

Besides, she had made it clear by her actions how she felt. He was going to have to be man enough to live with it.

Saturday dawned with clear skies and sunshine. A perfect day to snow-machine, Sharon commented at breakfast. Grant agreed, then retired to his den to work.

If questioned, he could have argued that he had a lot of work to do. But deep inside, he knew that he was hiding, from Sharon, from himself. And in recognizing that fact, he finally realized that he probably had used his work in the same manner in the past. Not to hide from Cassie but to control the feeling that his life had spun out of control with a disintegrating marriage, Catherine's illness and then raising a daughter on his own.

He'd been frightened. Overwhelmed. And... He sighed. It had been easier to deal with the demands of work, easier to provide things for Cassie, than to deal with a world shattered beyond recognition.

Shame rushed through him. Sickened, he dropped his pen and sat staring at the paperwork. And here he was again, burying himself in paperwork.

No, he thought, this was different. This was for Sharon's own good, the good of their marriage, because he had to get his desire under control. This was altogether different.

But... He squared his shoulders. He would never use his work like that again. He lifted his pen and started working once more.

Sharon went and picked up Cassie. An hour later, their chatter and laughter filled the house, drifting down the hall and into the den. Grant tried to concentrate. He gripped his pen tighter, hunched over the paperwork as if to protect it and tried to ignore the sound of Sharon's voice. Her laugh. A sound that twisted around him like a silken noose. Tugging. Tightening. Pulling him to her.

He should have made love to her last night. He had to do *something* to get her out of his system.

But he wouldn't have been able to live with himself afterward. Besides, he wasn't so sure that it would have worked. Wasn't so sure that it wouldn't have made him just want her more. A thought that disturbed him as much as the unwelcome desire.

Cassie shrieked with laughter, Brittany barked, then Sharon laughed. Grant put down his pen and accepted that he wasn't going to be able to work. That maybe what he needed was to spend more time with Sharon rather than less and kill the attraction with familiarity.

He went in search of his family. The three of them, four including Brittany, ended up in the garage getting the snow machines ready for an outing the next day.

The air was crisp and cold, even colder as it rushed past their faces as they sped up the frozen riverbed, the roar of the snow machines nearly deafening. Cassie perched in front of Grant in the two-up seat, sheltered by his arms and body. Though they bounced through ruts, flew over hills, she clung to his arms like a burr to a pony.

Sharon passed them with a flash of teeth behind her helmet shield and a cocky wave of hand. Grant couldn't help but smile back as he gripped the handlebars, opened up the gas and shot past her. She threw her head back and laughed, a laughter drowned by the roar of the machines, yet it reached out and touched Grant as if a physical touch.

Answering laughter welled up from within. And suddenly he felt more alive than he had in years.

They wound their way through icebergs held in the grip of the frozen river at the base of Valdez Glacier. Climbed the face of the glacier on a twisting trail that skirted crevasses of blue ice hundreds and hundreds of years old. The trail straightened, widened. Jagged, formidable peaks of snow and rock shaped a valley that the glacier spilled down, that they now climbed into as if climbing toward heaven.

Sun washed the snow, adding to the brilliance with a promise of warmth, in direct contrast to the chilled air. Clean-fresh air. Grant stopped his machine, cut the engine. Sharon did likewise, and suddenly they were engulfed in thick, cold silence. A silence that wasn't truly quiet but only seemed so because it was devoid of sounds of man, filled with the snap and crackle of sun against rock, against snow and ice. A breeze whispered along the peaks, through the valley.

Grant pulled off his helmet, dropped his head back and savored the feel of sun on his face. The bite of cold against his skin. When he looked, Sharon had done the same. Cheeks flushed, eyes shut. Curls dancing on the breeze.

Alive, the breeze seemed to whisper. *Alive.*

Every cell in his body responded to the whisper, invigorated. Grant knew he had Sharon to thank for the feeling, because without her prodding, without her presence in his house, he would be sitting in a stuffy den, working, hardly noticing the sunlight that streamed through the window.

Not only was she good for Cassie, becoming the mother his child so badly needed, she was also good for him. A loyal friend who staunchly defended him, even against himself.

Alive, the breeze whispered again. Grant threw back his head and laughed. Laughed for no other reason than it felt good, and he hadn't laughed enough the past few years.

Sharon went to Anchorage for a manager's meeting. Cassie cried when she left, then clung to Grant the balance of the evening. She immediately fell asleep when put to bed, exhausted from emotion spent.

Grant wandered through a house that suddenly seemed far too quiet. A house that had changed, he realized, walking from room to room. There were now splashes of color where throw pillows and afghans were flung. Rich bits of life hung on the wall. He studied the bright-eyed fox in the family room, smiling at the pup peeking from between her front legs. Clowns smiled or frowned, sat or danced, held balloons or only empty hands on the shelves where there had once been crystal.

He slowly walked down the hall, hesitated, then swung open the door to Sharon's room. A room that reflected her warm, down-to-earth personality. Several framed photos of Cassie sat perched on top of the dresser. Crayon drawings were pinned to one wall. Clearly this room belonged to someone who loved Cassie, loved children.

What was it that Dorothy had said? Something to the effect that she wished they would reconsider their decision not to have children...because they were wonderful parents. Dorothy was right. Sharon was great with Cassie.

He frowned and walked down the hall to his own room. Why had Sharon agreed to marry him, knowing there would be no children? Their entire childhood, she had often declared that she was going to have at least six children. Yet she and Charley had had none. And by marrying Grant, she had given up any hope for a family of her own.

Though he'd always been able to push the questions away, they now returned. When Sharon proposed they marry, she'd been adamant she did not want emotional involvement from a man. Been adamant that having Cassie was all the family she would need. Grant had bought into that argument because he was also committed to never becoming emotionally involved again.

But...for a woman like Sharon to give up the chance for more children... The more he thought about it, the more it just didn't make sense.

It's none of your business, he told himself as he undressed and slid beneath the covers.

The familiar silence of night, of a house when all the lights are shut off, the occupants in bed, settled around him. A silence that was oddly empty, almost as if the absence of Sharon had somehow taken something away.

The hustle and bustle of Anchorage was exhilarating. After the meetings the first day, Sharon hit her favorite shopping mall and bought books for Cassie, as well as some finger paints and art paper. Potpourri for the house. Dog treats for Brittany. And for Grant...she struggled over a beautiful wool shirt, dark navy and gray, that would wonderfully accentuate his eyes. In the end, she bought it.

The second evening was for herself. Dinner and a movie, after a quick trip to her favorite bookstore to stock up. The third day the meetings ended at noon. She made for the grocery store and discount stores and filled the extra suitcase she had brought, as well a large duffel. Then she headed for the airport, exhausted from meetings and shopping and traffic and wanting nothing more than to get home to her family.

Her breath caught at the thought. Then she smiled. Her family. Her family. She repeated it over and over in her mind. Sang it out loud, glad that no one else was in the rental car, and giggled. Her family.

It didn't matter that she loved Grant and could not tell him. It didn't matter that she fantasized about having her way with him. She could handle that, handle anything, because the price she paid was well worth those two small words that meant so very much.

Cassie danced from foot to foot in the doorway to the terminal, flung herself at Sharon, nearly knocking her down. Grant was smiling from ear to ear, a sight that had Sharon catching her breath and wishing with all her heart that she could be like Cassie and fling herself into Grant's arms.

Brittany yelped and danced a welcome as Sharon entered the house. "You would think I have been gone a year," she said, laughing and kneeling to fondle the pup.

"It felt like a year!" Cassie squeezed her neck tight. "Daddy couldn't even do a French braid," she complained.

"Hey." Grant raised his hands as if to defend himself. "It's not like I've had a lot of practice, you know." He ran his hand through his thick hair, tousling it. "French braids are for mothers to do."

Mothers. The word squeezed Sharon's heart, and she blinked back sudden tears of happiness. When her vision cleared, Grant was watching her with a frown.

Cassie cried with delight at her books and art supplies. Grant silently took the shirt. "You didn't—"

Sharon reached a finger to still his lips. "I wanted to," she said softly. "Okay?"

He hesitated, then nodded. "Yeah, okay."

He arched his brow, arched it even farther as Sharon unpacked her suitcase and duffel full of groceries and household items. "I thought the plane looked a little heavy trying to land," he said with a straight face. The twinkle in his eye gave him away.

After a quick dinner, they retired to the family room. Cassie grabbed a new book and snuggled next to Sharon on the couch. "Can you read it, please?"

"I think that can be managed," she said softly. She glanced over at Grant, caught him staring at the two of them, a frown creasing his brow. Her heart jumped a little. He half smiled when he realized she was looking at him, and turned his attention back to his book.

"Sharon?"

Cassie's hesitant voice pulled her attention back to the little girl. She plucked at Sharon's sleeve, a nervous gesture that made Sharon wary.

"Yes, Cass." She wondered with a leap of heart what was wrong. A deep frown creased Cassie's brow. Her eyes were downcast; her lower lip was caught between her teeth, deeply indented by the pressure.

Fear shot through Sharon. She could almost feel Grant's gaze, but kept her focus on Cassie. "Is everything okay, Cass?" she asked softly.

Cassie nodded, then released her lip with expelled breath. "I was...I mean... Well, I was wondering..." She hesitated.

Sharon wrapped an arm around her shoulder and waited, heart pounding louder in her chest.

Cassie swallowed, so hard Sharon could hear it. An ominous sound.

"Well, I was wondering...would it be okay if I called you 'Mom'?" she whispered.

Tears came to Sharon's eyes, as unexpected as Cassie's request. "Of course you can call me 'Mom,'" she said in a husky voice. Then she pulled the little girl hard against her with a hug.

"Not 'Mama,'" Cassie clarified. "Cause...well, cause—"

"That's special for Catherine," Sharon said. "I understand."

Cassie met her gaze, eyes serious. "Do you think Mama would care?"

Sharon smiled gently, too choked with emotion to speak. "No, I'm sure she wouldn't," she finally managed.

"I love you, Sha—Mom."

Cassie reached up and wound her arms around Sharon's neck and squeezed, a grip that made breathing nearly impossible. Breathing wasn't as important as the hug, as the little girl. As the sound of "Mom" on her lips—something she had been afraid to hope for. Her happiness was complete except for...Grant, she admitted with an inward sigh. If only she and Grant were a real husband and wife. But it was something she knew would not happen.

Sharon finally loosened the grip, slowly raised her gaze to meet Grant's. He smiled, but she sensed that something was bothering him.

A little later, Sharon tucked Cassie in, patted Brittany on the head and went back into the family room. Grant looked up from his book. "You don't mind that Cassie wants to call me 'Mom,' do you?" she asked.

"No," he said quietly.

She waited, thought he was going to say more.

Then he shook his head. "No, I don't mind. I'm glad."

"Well, then...I think I'll turn in." She started to leave the room.

"Sharon."

Grant's voice stopped her, drew her around. His dark eyes captured and held her. "It's good to have you back."

He said the words in a husky voice that seemed to reach out and run a light finger the length of her spine.

It was all that she could do to nod silently and turn to go, when what she really wanted was to pull Grant from his chair and walk hand in hand to his room.

The wind picked up that night, howling past the house, hammering the windows and rattling at the roof like a monster gone wild. Streets were polished to a sheen, reduced to near ice-rink conditions. Streets that cars crept along the following morning, studded tires and four-wheel drive not a match for what Mother Nature had dealt.

The wind had been gusting for days, rolling threatening black clouds in from the sea to fill the sky and settle over Valdez, obscuring the mountain peaks. Temperatures suddenly rose and by evening the clouds finally released their burden, a heavy patter of rain that turned streets, already dangerous, even more so. Water whooshed beneath tires as cars slid around corners or through stop signs. By dinner hour the roads were virtually deserted; those who could be were snugged in their homes, safe, warm and dry.

Cassie was restless. She wanted to go sledding. "It's too wet and too icy. It won't be good sledding," Sharon reminded her. The little girl pouted and started to whine.

"That will be enough," Grant admonished.

He shot a warning glance at Cassie, turned back to building a fire, wool shirt stretching across broad shoulders. The wool shirt she had bought him. Sharon's breath caught at the sight. She stilled a quickening of pulse.

Cassie chewed her lower lip, frowning. She eyed Grant, then Sharon. "Can me and Brittany go outside and play?"

Grant stood and arched a brow at Sharon. The kindling in the fire snapped and crackled behind him. Sharon shrugged, trying not to notice how the colors in the shirt deepened his eyes to an impossibly dark blue. Eyes she could easily get caught in.

"You'll have to stay out of the streets, period. I know we hardly ever get any traffic, but it's icy, dangerous. Don't even so much as touch a toe in them," Grant finally said.

"I won't, Daddy. I will stay in the next lot. Come on, Brit." Cassie raced off to get her winter gear on.

"And keep Brittany on her leash," Sharon called after her.

"I will," Cassie shouted back.

Sharon met Grant's gaze. "I think I'll sit in the living room, to keep a better eye on them." She gathered her book and settled on the living room couch, just able to see the lot in which Cassie and Brittany now bounced and rolled together in the glare of a streetlight. They climbed halfway down the snowbank, then scrambled back up, down and up, careful to stay out of the street.

A few minutes later, Grant walked in, book in hand. "Seems kind of quiet in there alone," he said, then settled in the chair, feet on the ottoman.

Warmth slid through Sharon. She snuggled beneath an afghan and opened her book.

The headlights came so swiftly that Sharon had only half risen when the brakes squealed and the car spun in circles at the end of the cul de sac, stopping, nose buried in the snowbank.

Grant beat Sharon to the front door, but only by inches.

The car engine died. Then Cassie shrieked, an unearthly scream that turned the blood in Sharon's veins to ice. The little girl huddled in the snowbank in front of the car, her cries filling the dark night.

Grant swore and raced across the ice, Sharon slipping and sliding at his heels, oblivious to the water that soaked her sock slippers, to the cold that numbed her feet.

"I didn't let her on the road. I didn't," Cassie moaned over and over as Grant gathered her in her arms. Brittany lay in a silent heap in the snow, rain flattening her fur, molding her still body, a trickle of blood at her mouth. Her leash trailed like a blue ribbon behind her.

The car door slammed. "I didn't mean... I mean, I couldn't help..." The youth's voice shook; his face was white.

"What the hell—" Grant put Cassie down and lunged, grabbing the boy by his collar.

"Grant!" Sharon raced forward. She slipped and fell, slamming into both of them, and they went down with a flounder of legs and arms on the watery ice.

Grant was the first to his feet. He towered over the boy, body shaking, hands fisted at his side, rage clearly etched on his hardened features, in his glittering eyes.

Sharon regained her feet, Cassie clinging to her hand. "I think we'd better call the police," she said.

Grant stared at her one long minute, then nodded, visibly reining in his anger.

"Stay with your dad," Sharon said to Cassie. Then she slowly walked over to the snowbank, climbed up to Brittany's still form. Tears blurred her vision as she reached to settle her hand against the pup she loved so well, her heart breaking.

The ribs rose beneath her hand. She gasped. They rose again, a slight movement but real. "Grant, quick, call the vet," she screamed.

He started to turn, then shrugged out of his shirt and threw it to her. Then he and Cassie raced for the house, with the youth left standing in the middle of the road.

Sharon tucked the wool shirt around the pup, tried to shelter her body from the rain and prayed.

Brittany had cracked ribs and a concussion. She'd been knocked out by the blow, and the blood had come from her biting her tongue. "We'll hold her here a couple of days to keep on eye on her," the vet said. "She should be good as new once those ribs heal," she reassured a hollow-eyed Cassie.

Grant thanked the woman once more, then ushered both Sharon and Cassie out to the pickup. It was a quiet trip home. Cassie slumped against Sharon, wrapped against her by a protective arm. Sharon's eyes were shadowed, slightly swollen from tears.

He would do anything for both of them, he realized. Even Sharon. The thought gave pause. He gripped the steering wheel tighter. It wasn't that he loved her. But she was the best friend he had, a woman who gave generously of her heart. Someone who deserved to have any and every happiness she desired.

You can't make anyone happy. Sharon's words. Words he had finally come to believe, at least in part. His eyes narrowed as they turned up the hill toward the house, water swooshing beneath the tires. He might not be able to make Sharon happy, but he would do his damnedest to help, to contribute to that happiness. Because she deserved it.

The garage door opened with a yawn. Both pickup doors slammed. Grant swept a half-asleep Cassie into his arms, Sharon at his heels. They tucked the little girl in, then walked into the hall together.

"It could have been Cassie," Sharon said in a weary voice.

Her eyes glittered with emotion when they met his. He didn't say a word, just stepped forward and folded her in his arms. She relaxed against him, and they stood as such for a couple of minutes.

Her head nested against his shoulder. He tucked his chin to bury his face in soft curls that smelled of rain and faintly of lemon-scented shampoo. She sighed and rubbed her cheek against his shoulder. He dropped a kiss to her brow.

They froze, carefully stepped apart, gazes locked. And suddenly the reasons they shouldn't didn't matter. He whispered her name in a hoarse voice. And then they were in each other's arms again. Hearts pounding, hands roaming, lips greedy and grasping as their need raced out of control.

There was no hesitation when Grant picked her up into his arms kicked the door open to her bedroom, their need greater than they. The door swung closed behind them. Clothes fell to the floor, and rational thought dissipated as bare skin met bare skin. Someone moaned. They tore at each other, starved, eager, caught in a maelstrom of emotion far stronger than they'd ever imagined.

When it was over, when they lay spent, side by side, Grant closed his mind to recrimination and pulled Sharon close. They slid beneath the soft quilt and slept, exhausted by the events of the days, satiated.

Sharon awoke first, her body curled against Grant's, held tight against him by his arm. Her breath caught as her first reaction was to flee. But she lingered, savoring the feel of his skin next to hers. The scent. The sight of his bare chest, quilt pulled to just above his navel and only to her waist.

These were things she had only dreamed of, never thinking they would be real, never daring to hope or believe that one day she would wake up in his arms. Knowing that it wouldn't last made it all the more special.

She should have been chilled. She wasn't. He slept on his back, hand cupping her shoulder, the other lying across his flat stomach. She resisted the urge to reach out and trace the long, tapering fingers, and flushed at the memory of what those fingers had done last night.

She knew it shouldn't have happened, and wouldn't again. But for the moment she simply could not bring herself to regret even a second of it.

Grant stirred. She could tell the second he was awake by the sudden stillness of his body. His fingers seemed to carefully relax their hold, to release her shoulder. He slowly pulled away, up into a sit, then swung himself to the edge of the bed.

She quickly turned, scrambled for her clothes, knowing with certainty his eyes did not follow. When she was dressed, she handed him his clothes and looked away while he dressed. She turned back when she sensed he was finished.

His eyes were dark, shuttered. Her heart sank, just a bit, then she straightened her shoulders.

"I know you didn't want that to happen. I'm sorry," Grant finally said, words careful.

"I'm not." Sharon met his startled gaze. "I won't be sorry for something we both wanted. Two mature, responsible adults." She swallowed hard. "Certainly it shouldn't have happened, but I won't be made to feel guilty, to feel as though we've done something wrong, when we haven't.

"We all make mistakes in life," she continued, "but I won't have you blaming me or blaming yourself for last night. I won't."

"I don't want emotional involvement," he said in a husky voice, though his eyes revealed no emotion.

"You don't have it," she lied. He would never know

she loved him. She lifted her chin. "I don't expect you to safeguard my happiness, if that is what you are thinking. And I don't expect to mean anything more to you than what I did before last night."

Silence surrounded them as Grant studied her. Then he nodded, once, turned and left the room. Sharon expelled pent-up breath, sank to the bed. She would not regret making love to Grant, she told herself with a fierceness that surprised her.

She'd waited a lifetime for this, and she would be damned if she would be sorry.

Chapter Ten

Grant cursed himself with every vile name he could think of. Sharon might not blame him, but he sure as hell did. He should have pulled back. Walked away. Instead—

He curled his hands at his side, unable to complete the thought. He strode into the bathroom, ripped off his clothes and stepped into the shower. Hot streams of water cascaded over his body but couldn't erase the memory of Sharon's hands.

Panic welled up within. He slammed his mind against the memory, swore to himself over and over. The last thing he needed was to do what he did to Sharon last night. The next to the last thing he needed was to face her over breakfast, or dinner, or anything, because he had let her down. He'd taken advantage of her vulnerability and he was not sure he could forgive himself for that.

He had to face her again. Otherwise she would think he was blaming her, something that was utterly untrue. He assumed full responsibility for their actions.

Slowly, carefully, he pulled at his emotions, until he had

them under full control. Then he stepped from the shower, toweled down and dressed. He glanced into the mirror over the dresser as he ran a comb through his hair. A cold, solitary man looked back. The man he'd been when he married Sharon. The man he had to be to stay married to her.

What if she was pregnant? His mouth dropped open at the thought. He whirled, unable to face himself.

She would want the child. He knew that without question.

She wasn't pregnant, he told himself.

But she could be, doubt whispered.

Breakfast was a silent affair. Even Cassie seemed subdued, probably because Brittany wasn't there. She finished her pancakes, excused herself and left the room.

The silence was almost overwhelming and stretched frayed nerves. Sharon pushed back her plate, unable to finish. "Maybe I'll call the vet and see if we can visit. That might cheer Cassie up." She started toward the phone.

"Sharon."

Grant's quiet voice stopped her midstep. Her heart dropped at the serious tone. She turned toward him.

"We didn't use protection last night." He stated the obvious, then continued before she could speak. "If you are pregnant—"

"I'm not." She snapped the words, a wave of panic sweeping her. He arched a brow. "I'm not," she repeated, then turned.

"Would it be that awful?"

The quiet question shocked her. She whirled, mouth open.

She closed her mouth, legs trembling so bad it was a wonder she could still stand. "I am not pregnant and I

won't be, so it isn't an issue," she finally managed. And
then she fled the room before he could say anything further. The last thing she wanted to hear was that Grant
wanted more children, because she would have to tell him.
And endure his pity. A pity she feared would soon turn to
rejection.

Hot and cold fear rushed through her at the thought that
she would lose Grant if he found out. Yet she knew she
would have to be honest if he pressed. She prayed he
would drop the subject.

Grant felt as though he had been kicked in the stomach
as Sharon hurried from the kitchen. Guilt swept him, so
strong he could not move, could not speak. She *did* want
children. The pain in her eyes, the panic in her voice...

Selfish bastard that he was, he had denied...was denying
Sharon something that she very much wanted to have.
Nausea rolled in his stomach. He swallowed hard and
briefly closed his eyes.

He sat frozen in thought for a long time. Trying to sort
the emotion that rolled through his gut, tied knots,
twisted—emotion he thought he had under control. Trying
to make some sense of the chaotic thoughts that raced
through his mind. Trying to make some sense of his life
that suddenly felt tilted on its axis, ready to tumble over
into disaster.

Finally, he stood, walked slowly from the room in
search of Sharon. He found her in her room, back to the
door, sitting on the bed, staring out the window. He
stepped inside and closed the door. She stiffened but did
not turn. He walked over to settle on the bed next to her,
and tried not to remember what had happened there just a
few short hours ago.

"We need to talk," he said quietly.

"I told you—"

"I know what you said." He paused, swallowed hard again, then continued. "We could have children, Sharon." She didn't say a word, didn't even look at him. "I mean...well... You're a natural, Sharon. You were meant to be a mother if anyone was. I would like to...I want to give you the children you want. The children you deserve."

She stared at him, eyes wide.

He forced himself to continue. "I know we don't love each other, but we care. Can't that be enough?"

"No," she cried. She buried her face in her hands, head bent, thick curls hiding her face. Then she looked over at him, tears shimmering in her eyes, face pale. "You said you didn't want more children," she half whispered.

He started to speak.

"I am so sorry, Grant. So very sorry. But I can't... I can't have children."

He paled, his eyes filling with concern.

"I am sorry I didn't tell you," she murmured hoarsely.

Grant couldn't believe what he was hearing. *I can't have children.* Each word was a stab of disbelief, of anger, of pain for Sharon, because if he ever knew a woman who should...who deserved children, it was her.

"Please don't look at me like that." Her voice trembled.

He reached for her without thought. "I'm sorry—"

"I don't want your pity." She jerked away, stood to face him, chin lifted. "And I will understand if you want to...divorce me."

"Divorce?" he said quietly.

She slowly nodded. "I should have told you that I'm...I am not...whole." She sucked in her breath. "I am only half a woman. Ask Charley."

He swore—a vile, filthy oath. "What would that little worm know?"

"That little worm, as you call him, knows what it's like

to be tied to a woman who can't give you what you want most—children.''

"Children," he repeated. "What about love? He didn't want that?"

Now she swallowed hard. He forced himself to remain seated, not go to her.

"Apparently love doesn't survive the disappointment of learning that the woman you married isn't as… Isn't a 'real woman,' I believe is the term he used." Pain darkened her eyes at the memory. Her cheeks flushed.

He sprang to his feet, anger surging through him. "If he were here, I'd kill him." He reached out and dragged Sharon to him, until she stood inches from him, as if closeness could make his words penetrate. "The man was…*is* a fool. He didn't know what he was talking about."

"He wanted children," she said quietly.

"Children." He spit the word as if it were a curse. "We don't always get what we want in life. He should have faced up to it, dealt with it."

"Like Catherine?" she asked softly.

His breath caught. "They aren't so very different," she continued. "They thought they needed something that each of us couldn't give them to be happy. Charley couldn't stand the thought of being married to me after he found out I was unable to have a child. Could hardly bear to touch me." She tried to smile and failed. "I will never, never put myself in that position again. Ever."

"Like Catherine?"

Her eyes widened at his question.

"Well?" He continued. "You told me that I wasn't responsible for her happiness, yet you seem to have assumed responsibility for Charley's."

"This is different," she argued. "It's—"

"No, it really isn't. Charley could have stayed. He should have." Grant drew a deep breath. "If there is one thing you have helped me see, it's that we are all responsible for dealing with what life has handed us. I wasn't...am not guilty of making Catherine miserable. She did it to herself. And you aren't putting yourself in that position again," he said with quiet assurance. "I don't need more children."

He cupped her jaw with his hand to keep her gaze. "And I can tell you without any shadow of doubt that Charley was—is—a damned fool. Because it wasn't half a woman who shared that bed with me last night. And if I ever...ever," he repeated, voice growing husky, "hear you say that again, I will bring you back in here and prove to you that you are all woman. A woman any man in his right mind would be proud—would be lucky—to call his wife."

"But—"

"But nothing." He arched a brow and nodded toward the bed. She blushed. "Well?" he challenged, tracing her jaw with a finger. "Are you going to believe me...or not?"

A half smile curved the corners of her mouth. Tears suddenly shimmered in her eyes. "Believe you, I suppose," she said in a husky voice.

He fought the urge to step forward and take her in his arms. Because if he did, they might very well end up in the bed they stood next to. And he didn't want to take advantage of Sharon in the vulnerable state she was in.

Sharon couldn't look away, every nerve in her body trembling. From Grant's touch. His words. His angry, adamant defense of her. His anger convinced her that he meant every word he said. That and the fact that she trusted him, a trust that was as much a part of her as breathing or the blood running in her veins. Grant would not lie to her. Each of his words had hammered at her fears, her doubts, shattering her insecurities. He truly felt that way. And...he was right. Charley could have stayed. They could have been happy together. It wasn't a failing on her part.

She took a deep breath, felt cleansed, somehow strengthened. The impossible happened. Her love for Grant swelled and rushed through her, larger and stronger than she'd ever thought possible.

She knew then that she would not be able to hide her feelings. She had to tell him the truth so that they could live with the reality. Regardless of the consequences.

She took a deep breath, then reached to cup his jaw. "I love you," she whispered.

His eyes widened with shock. He took a quick step back and swore. "That isn't what this is all about. Isn't—"

"I know," she gently interrupted, recognizing panic in his voice. "It has nothing to do with what you just said, or even last night. I have loved you all my life. And when you didn't notice, I loved you as a friend, Grant. When I suggested we marry, I didn't realize I still loved you. But now I know I did."

His eyes suddenly hardened. His mouth thinned; his jaw tensed. The transformation was almost frightening as he became a Grant she didn't know.

"I am not asking for your love in return," she added softly.

"I don't want your love." He carefully enunciated the words, then spun on his heel and left.

The cold words hurt—she couldn't deny that. But the pain was tempered by recognition that Grant was terrified. Pure and simple. And he was running in the only way he knew how. By turning cold and hard. And yet, by running, did that mean he felt more than he knew? Dared she hope?

No. She answered her own question. If over time Grant grew to love her, she would welcome that love. But she knew it might not ever happen. Knew that she would have to learn to be happy with what she had. And she would have to prove to him that it was enough for her. Enough for her and something that he could live with.

She ached to go after him, to help, but realized he needed time alone. As did she. She smoothed the quilt and trembled at the memory of Grant's lovemaking. A memory that swept heat through her body. Would that one memory be enough? Could she live without ever experiencing being in his arms again?

She didn't think so. And wasn't sure what to do about it.

Fury fueled his steps. Grant strode out to the pickup, suddenly needing nothing worse than to get away from the house, the confining walls, from Sharon.

But he couldn't escape the memory of her words.

He gripped the steering wheel as he wheeled out of the garage and down the road. She loved him. He swore and slammed the palm of his hand against the steering wheel. How could things have gone this far? He'd told her he didn't want emotional involvement and yet that is exactly what they had now.

He sped out of town in the pickup, heading away from his house, away from Sharon. He drew a deep breath, getting a handle on the panic. The anger that was already subsiding.

What crime had Sharon really committed by caring for Cassie, loving her as if she were her own? By staunchly defending Grant against himself, while forcing him to face his past? By helping to heal the breach with Hugh and Dorothy? By making his home a warm, happy place, which drew him each evening to leave work as early as possible? By encouraging him to live a whole well-rounded life once more?

He sighed and slowed the pickup. She certainly was a

terrible person, he thought with a half smile, the remnant of panic and anger dying. There ought to be a law.

Yet he didn't want Sharon's love. Didn't want the burden of her happiness—

The memory of her words stopped the thought. He wasn't responsible for anyone's happiness. And she certainly seemed able to make her own. She had survived a callous divorce—something that would have embittered many people. Survived the disappointment of not being able to have children. Again, an embittering experience for some. Instead, she'd opened up her heart to Cassie, and made both their lives whole, more complete.

And though he hadn't wanted to hear the words, he had to hand it to her. The woman was honest to the bone. He pulled over to the side of the road, leaned his head against the steering wheel and thought. Long and hard.

About the woman brave enough to take on a sour, lonely man and his daughter. A woman strong enough to deal with Cassie's initial rejection. To reach out to Hugh and Dorothy when they could have easily rejected her. A woman who made love to him with a fervor he had never experienced before.

She loved him. And he was running again. Running from Sharon or running from himself? He wasn't sure. A knot tightened in his stomach. A semi roared by.

His mind circled the truth. The truth that whispered, called out to him, until he finally allowed it to be. Forced himself to face it. He loved her.

The knot in his stomach loosened just a bit, even as he denied the thought.

And why else would he offer to give her what he felt she wanted most—children? Why wasn't he happy with the belief that he'd found the perfect mother for Cassie without any emotional attachment on his part? Why was he drawn home earlier and earlier each evening? Drawn to spend time with, be in the same room with, make love to Sharon? Why did the thought of never making love to Sharon hurt so damned much he could hardly stand it?

Because he loved her, and he was too big a fool, too frightened, to see. With truth came strength. Grant straightened, pulled back out on the road, then drove until he could turn around.

He loved Sharon, and he'd just taken the love she'd offered and brutally rejected it. He swallowed hard and wondered how he was going to explain, how he was going to make her believe that he truly did love her.

By the time Grant got home, his nerves were stretched so taut he almost expected them to snap. His throat was dry, his heart pounding with fear. What if she rejected him? Maybe she already regretted confessing her love. Decided it was a mistake.

He rushed through the house, rounded the corner of Sharon's room and stopped midstep. She was packing. Carefully pulling her clothes from her dresser, stacking them neatly on the bed. Leaving him. His heart slammed into his throat.

"Sharon." Her name was more a cry, a husky plea.

She whirled, hand flying to her chest. "You scared me half to death," she gasped.

He didn't answer, couldn't find the words, and cursed himself his inability.

Their gazes locked. She lifted her chin. He took a step closer.

"Don't leave," he whispered hoarsely.

"Leave?" Her eyes widened. "I'm not leaving. I'm moving into your room."

He gaped.

She ignored him, words rushing from her. "There is no reason we can't live together as man and wife, even if you don't love me in the same way that I love you. I know you care, Grant. If that is enough for me, can't it be for you?'' She paused briefly, cheeks suddenly flushed. ''I know you...want me. That you find me—''

''Stop,'' he said quietly. Her cheeks paled, her shoulders stiffened. He walked forward, tilted her chin with a finger. ''I thought you were leaving me.''

''I would never leave you,'' she said without hesitating.

He smiled then, heart swelling with love. ''That's good, because I don't intend to let you.'' Her eyes widened, full of questions. He reached to drop a gentle kiss on her lips, then rested his brow against hers. His heart was so full of emotion, he could hardly breathe. Hardly speak.

''I love you,'' he murmured.

She pulled away to stare at him. ''You don't have to say—''

''The only thing I have to do is love you,'' he said softly. ''I can't help it, so you will just have to make do.'' He lowered his lips to hers in a kiss he made certain would leave little doubt about his love.

''Daddy! What are you doing?'' Cassie cried out.

Grant turned to face his daughter, arm tight around Sharon's shoulders. ''I am kissing your mom. You got a problem with that?''

Cassie frowned, then shook her head. ''No, but could you hurry up. I wanta go visit Brittany.''

He arched a brow toward Sharon. She stood on tiptoe to brush a kiss across his lips. ''I think we could hurry this time. We have the rest of our lives,'' she said softly.

''Yeah, I guess we do,'' Grant answered. But he lowered his lips to hers for one more lingering kiss.

''The rest of our lives,'' he repeated.

*   *   *   *   *

Bestselling author

JOAN JOHNSTON

continues her wildly popular miniseries with an
all-new, longer-length novel

The Virgin Groom

HAWK'S WAY

One minute, Mac Macready was a living legend in
Texas—every kid's idol, every man's envy, every
woman's fantasy. The next, his fiancée dumped him,
his career was hanging in the balance and his future
was looking mighty uncertain. Then there was the
matter of his scandalous secret, which didn't stand a
chance of staying a secret. So would he succumb to
Jewel Whitelaw's shocking proposal—or take cold
showers for the rest of the long, hot summer…?

Available August 1997
wherever Silhouette books are sold.

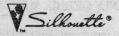

Silhouette®

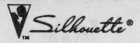

Wanted: Brides! This small South Dakota town
needs women of marriageable age. And
Silhouette Romance invites you to visit the
handsome, extremely eligible men of:

a new miniseries by
Sandra Steffen

♥ The local veterinarian finds himself falling for his feisty
receptionist—the one woman in town *not* interested in
finding herself a husband.

LUKE'S WOULD-BE BRIDE
(June '97)

♥ This sheriff's got a reputation for being the good guy, yet a
certain single gal has him wanting to prove just what a wolf in
sheep's clothing he really is.

WYATT'S MOST WANTED WIFE
(August '97)

♥ A rugged rancher proposes a marriage of convenience to a
dowdy diner waitress, but just wait till his ugly-duckling
bride turns into a swan.

CLAYTON'S MADE-OVER MRS.
(October '97)

Don't miss any of these wonderful love stories, available only from

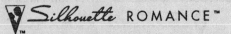

**Beginning in September
from Silhouette Romance...**

a new miniseries by
Carolyn Zane

They're a passel of long, tall, swaggering cowboys who need tamin'...and the love of a good woman. So y'all come visit the brood over at the Brubaker ranch and discover how these rough and rugged brothers got themselves hog-tied and hitched to the marriage wagon.

The fun begins with
MISS PRIM'S UNTAMABLE COWBOY (9/97)

"No little Miss Prim is gonna tame me! I'm not about to settle down!"
   —Bru "nobody calls me Conway" Brubaker
"Wanna bet?"
   —Penelope Wainwright, a.k.a. Miss Prim

The romance continues in
HIS BROTHER'S INTENDED BRIDE (12/97)

"Never met a woman I couldn't have...then I met my brother's bride-to-be!"
   —Buck Brubaker, bachelor with a problem
"Wait till he finds out the wedding was never really on...."
   —the not-quite-so-engaged Holly Fergusson

**And look for Mac's story coming in early '98 as
THE BRUBAKER BRIDES series continues, only from**

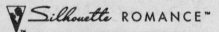